WILDERNESS JOURNEY

WILDERNESS JOURNEY

Ruth Nulton Moore

Illustrated by Allan Eitzen

HERALD PRESS
Scottdale, Pennsylvania
Kitchener, Ontario
1979

Library of Congress Cataloging in Publication Data

Moore, Ruth Nulton.
  Wilderness journey.

  SUMMARY: Two Scotch-Irish boys travel across
Pennsylvania in 1799 with a circuit-riding preacher to
search for their mother whom they expect to find in
Pittsburgh working and getting a home ready for them.
  [1. Pennsylvania—Fiction. 2. Adventure stories]
I. Eitzen, Allan. II. Title.
PZ7.M7878Wi   [Fic]   79-20489
ISBN 0-8361-1906-1
ISBN 0-8361-1907-X pbk.

WILDERNESS JOURNEY
Copyright © 1979 by Herald Press, Scottdale, Pa. 15683
  Published simultaneously in Canada by Herald Press,
  Kitchener, Ont. N2G 4M5
Library of Congress Catalog Card Number: 79-20489
International Standard Book Numbers:
  0-8361-1906-1 (hardcover)
  0-8361-1907-X (softcover)
Printed in the United States of America
Design: Alice B. Shetler

15 14 13 12 11 10 9 8 7 6 5 4 3 2 1

To
Mildred I. Moore,
who first told me the story
of James and John Graham,
and to
Gladys W. Hufford,
who has done so much to kindle my
interest in early Western Pennsylvania history

CONTENTS

LEAVING FOR AMERICA

JAMES GRAHAM sat up in bed and rubbed his eyes. He was startled to see a dark shadow outlined against the early morning gray of the window. The shadow moved toward the bed and the next moment he felt a hand touch his shoulder.

"Jamie, are you awake?" It was his mother's hushed voice.

James nodded and yawned, his head still full of dreams.

"It's time to get up," Mother's voice spoke again. "Wake your brother and hurry. You know how slow he is getting around in the morning."

"But Mother, it's not even daylight," James started

to protest. Then as Mother's dark shadow moved away from the bed, he suddenly remembered. How could he have forgotten!

He rolled over in bed and shook the sleeping form of his younger brother next to him.

"Johnny, Johnny, wake up!"

With a groan John rolled over and buried his head deeper under the covers, mumbling, "It's not time to get up yet, Jamie. It's not even daylight and I didn't hear the cock crow—"

Before he could drop off to sleep again, James gave his brother another shake. "We must get up this minute. Father and Uncle Alex will have the wagon ready and we mustn't make them wait. Don't you know what day this is?"

John struggled to a sitting position, blinking his eyes and shaking his head thoughtfully. Then it all came back to him. His father's return last night from Belfast. The exciting news that he had found passage on a sailing ship bound for America and that they would be leaving today.

For a long time Father had talked about taking his family to America where so many Ulstermen were making new homes. Father had told them, "Our countrymen want to leave the political unrest we have here in Northern Ireland. They want to live in a country where they can worship God as they please and at the same time live in peace with their neighbors."

Both James and John well remembered the terrible Irish rebellion last year in Ulster, when friends and neighbors of different faiths fought against one another. Even though the fighting was over, there was still so much hatred and suspicion.

Their neighbor, Malcolm McPherson, had sailed to America with his family last year. He had written Father a long letter about the American frontier in the Ohio Valley where he had taken his family to settle. There were many acres of good, rich land there, just waiting for families to come and settle on it. He had bought more acres than he was able to farm alone and had urged Father to come to America and share his land with him.

"Malcolm wrote that land is cheap on the American frontier," Father had told them after he had read the letter. "In a few years, with you lads to help me, I could earn enough money to pay Malcolm for the land we farm and then it will be ours."

"But you are a weaver, James," Mother had protested. "You are not a farmer."

"Aye, but the price of wool here in County Antrim is so high that I cannot buy enough that is needed for my loom," Father had replied with a sigh. Then he raised his head and squared his shoulders. "If Malcolm Mc-Pherson can learn to be a farmer in America, so can I."

At first Mother was reluctant to leave Ireland, but after she had prayed about the matter, she finally agreed that it might be best for them to make a new home in a land where there was peace and opportunity.

All that winter their father had worked hard at his loom to earn enough money for the passage to America. He was a fine weaver and he assured Mother that when they arrived in Philadelphia, he could earn the money they would need to buy a horse and wagon to travel the three hundred miles to the Ohio Valley.

11

James was proud of their adventuresome, hard-working father. Now as he struggled into his shirt, his heart beat fast. Today, April 1, 1799, they would be leaving for America.

His brother's laughing voice broke into his thoughts. "You must have my shirt, Jamie."

John slipped the loose woven garment back over his head and tossed it across the bed to where James sat dressing.

"Aye, the one I have on does feel a wee bit tight," James replied. "It's not light enough to see whose shirt is whose."

James was fourteen, two years older than his brother. He had his father's light-brown hair and quiet, serious manner. John had red hair and freckles, like Mother, and her gay, lighthearted ways.

When they were dressed, the brothers hurried down to the kitchen where Mother had a hasty breakfast ready for them. While they ate their porridge and drank their tea, they watched her finish her packing.

"I've left these till last," Mother told them as she took the family treasure from its place of honor on top of the sideboard. They were six of the king's silver spoons that her grandmother in Scotland had given to her as a wedding present. Mother's blue eyes always lighted up with pride when she looked at the silver spoons. Now the boys watched her slender hands wrap the spoons carefully in a linen cloth and place them between the clothing in the big leather trunk.

"There," Mother said, "now Father can close the lid and fasten the brass lock."

After that, things began to happen so quickly that it seemed to the boys, when they looked back on it later, that they had been living in a dream. Suddenly the little kitchen was filled with relatives and friends who had come to see them off and wish them a safe journey. There was Uncle Thomas, a weaver, who had bought the house and Father's loom. There was Uncle Alex, who was to take them to Belfast. There was Grandmother Ewart, with tears in her eyes as she kissed each one of them good-bye.

At last they were ready to leave. Mother looked back at the cozy little kitchen with a sigh and Father glanced for the last time at his big loom, standing in the corner by the hearth.

James's eyes followed his father's. The heavy wooden frame by the hearth seemed to be part of the family and James knew how his father must feel leaving it behind. Father had been teaching him how to weave and James now imagined himself sitting on the bench, tossing the shuttle back and forth over the warp. For a fleeting moment the steady clack, clack of the loom filled his ears. He would never forget that familiar, comforting sound.

John ran out the door ahead of the others. He did not look back at the cozy little house or Father's loom. He ran straight to his Uncle Alex's wagon where the old horse, Angus, stood waiting patiently with lowered head. John remembered the good times he had whenever he visited his uncle's farm and he rode the old gray horse.

He wanted to say good-bye to Angus now, for there might not be time to say good-bye in Belfast. He reached up and patted the horse's gray muzzle. "Good-bye, Old Angus," he whispered sadly. "I wish I could take you with me to ride in America."

The horse nickered softly and nuzzled the top of the boy's red head. John swallowed hard as a lump rose in his throat. Then he was aware that his family was gathered around the wagon and everybody was saying good-bye. Father laid a hand on his shoulder and motioned for him to climb into the wagon bed next to his brother. Then he and Uncle Alex lifted the big leather trunk into the back of the wagon.

Uncle Alex climbed up on the wagon seat and Father climbed up beside him. Mother sat in the back with the two boys. Uncle Alex picked up the reins and clucked at Old Angus and the younger, chestnut mare by his side.

"Good-bye, good-bye," called everyone.

James glanced down at Grandmother Ewart, whom they would probably never see again, and a sadness welled up inside him at the sight of the frail old lady.

The wagon wheels started turning and down the road they went. Tears sparkled in Mother's eyes as she waved a last farewell to her mother. Grandmother Ewart waved back, then putting her handkerchief to her eyes, she turned and went into the empty house.

For most of the day they rode through the dark glens and past the familiar green peat bogs of County Antrim. They passed stone houses with thatched roofs and gray plumes of smoke, from peat fires inside, drifting from the stone chimneys. They passed small green pastures with mossy stone fencerows and here and there a desolate moor covered with sparse heather.

When at last they came within sight of the Belfast hills, Father turned and called back to them. "We'll soon be there!"

14

The black cliffs dipped down to the coast. When James first caught sight of the sea, he nudged John excitedly and pointed to the waves that broke against the towering black rocks in great sprays of foam.

A sudden spring rain began to fall as they rode through the narrow, crowded streets of Belfast. Mother wrapped her shawl over her head and the boys pulled their woolen caps down over their ears to keep dry. But when they reached the quay, they forgot about the rain as they stared at the many ships in port. Some had their sails unfurled, ready to sail. Others with sails furled formed a forest of masts and spars along the waterfront.

"Which one are we sailing to America on?" John asked eagerly.

"You will see it tomorrow," Father told him. "We will board at daybreak."

Father guided Uncle Alex toward a small inn far down the quay, where they would be spending the night. As they rode along the docks, they passed ships of all sizes and from all nations. On one, sailors were swabbing the deck and singing at their work. On another, a man, as agile as a monkey, was climbing a tall mast to the masthead high above. They rode under the shadow of elaborately carved figureheads displayed below the bowsprit of the larger ships. The smells of the waterfront—salty, tarry, and spicy—made the boys' nostrils quiver with delight.

"Look!" John nudged his brother and pointed to a brown-faced sailor with rings in his ears and a long tarred pigtail. With a rolling gait, the sailor ambled up to a tavern and opened the door. Inside, the smoky air echoed with a loud sea chantey.

15

To the two country boys who had never seen the sea before, these new sights and smells and sounds were a delight. And they whispered to each other as they rode along the quay that they couldn't wait until tomorrow when they would be sailing on one of these tall ships, with a piping bosun and pigtailed sailors, to a new home across the sea.

STORM AT SEA

"HEAVE HO, Mister Hobbs!" commanded the captain. "Heave away!"

At the shrill piping of the bosun's whistle, the crew at the capstan turned the windlass to hoist anchor. It was early morning and they were sailing with the tide.

James and John leaned against the lee rail and watched the anchor come up, dripping by the side of the bow. Above them sailors were climbing the ratlines to the yards. The two boys listened to the shouting hustle of the crew aloft as the sails unfurled.

"Royals up, sir!"

"Top gallant up!"

One by one the sails unfurled: the topsails, the foresail, the mainsail, the crossjack sail, the spanker in the stern, and the three jibs over the bow. The sails caught the wind and billowed out. There was a sudden tilt of the deck, then a steady lift and roll as the prow cut through the water and the ship heeled gracefully to the wind. They were on their way!

As they sailed out of Belfast Lough and into the North Channel, the boys stood close together on deck, gazing aloft through a maze of ropes and tackle to where the white canvas sails snapped and billowed in the wind.

Father had joined Mother in their cabin in the steerage, but the boys were too excited to leave deck. Careful to keep out of the crew's way, they hugged the rail and watched the land slip away. Now only the black cliffs of Belfast, still partly wreathed with morning mist, could be seen off to the west.

They were at sea at last, sailing down the North Channel to the Irish Sea and then on into the broad Atlantic Ocean. Now and then they caught glimpses of land as they sailed south along the eastern coast of Ireland.

"That be Ards Peninsula in County Down, lads," a passing mate told them, pointing to the distant shore. " 'Twill be the last land ye'll be seein' for a while, so take a good long look."

Quietly the boys watched the shoreline become fainter and fainter, each saying his own silent good-bye to Ireland. James thought of Uncle Alex and Grandmother Ewart somewhere in that distant landscape and felt a sudden twinge of sadness. He knew how much Grandmother would be missing them that day and for many days to come.

They watched the last of the land fade away and when they could see it no longer, they made their way down the hatch to the steerage below.

Their quarters were small with a top bunk for the boys to sleep in and a lower one for Mother and Father. Their big leatherbound trunk took up the rest of the space in the tiny cabin so that there was just barely enough room to walk around in. Father was sitting on the lower berth with Mother, who was busily knitting by his side. Mother always knitted fast when something bothered her, and James supposed that this new experience at sea, with the rocking ship and the excited calls of the crew, did worry her somewhat. Her knitting needles fairly flew.

"Well, lads, what do you think of the ship?" asked Father.

"She seems a clever craft," John answered brightly.

James nodded and, although he had no further reply, his blue eyes were sparkling.

"I wish I could get used to this rolling motion," Mother said as she stood up unsteadily to get something out of the trunk.

Her face was pale and Father suggested that a stroll around the upper deck would do her good. "It'll help you get your sea legs, Mary," he said.

So, helping Mother up the hatchway, they joined the passengers and crew on deck. The passage down the North Channel was always a bit rough, a brown old sailor with hair bleached white from the sun told them. But when they reached the Atlantic, and if the weather stayed calm, the sailing would be easier. His assurance and the brisk, cool sea air brightened Mother's spirits a bit. She was even able to drink some tea and eat a sea biscuit that night for supper.

When they reached the open sea, the old sailor's prediction came true. On calm, bright days, it was a pleasure to be on deck and fill their lungs with tangy sea air.

The boys soon became used to the steady lift and roll of the ship and spent as much time as they could on deck. They liked to sit on coils of rope during the dogwatch in the late afternoon and listen to the sea chanteys the sailors sang while they washed or mended their clothes. Sometimes they watched the helmsman at the wheel as he steered the ship or they'd climb the quarterdeck to watch the ship's wake make a long foamy furrow across the green water. And, if they felt hungry, they'd scrounge a piece of cheese fron the cook.

At night in their cabin, they would talk about their new home in America. Father had sent a letter to Malcolm McPherson last winter when they had first decided to leave Ireland. And Malcolm had sent them a letter in return which instructed Father how to go about getting a wagon and team to take them over the Pennsylvania mountains to the Ohio Valley.

Malcolm had drawn a rough map for Father to follow, marking the places along the mountain road where they could find lodging or camp for the night. When they reached the town of Pittsburgh, at the end of their journey, Father was to inquire at the land office where they might find Malcolm's claim.

To Father the sea voyage seemed to take forever, he was so anxious to reach America. "After I pay the land off," he said, "I'll buy a loom and we'll start weaving again, Jamie."

20

Little did they know, as they talked happily about their new home in America, how changed their lives would soon become. Later, as James thought back on it, the trouble seemed to have come with the storm at sea.

They had been on the ocean only a week when one morning they awoke to the horrible pitching of the vessel in steep green seas.

The timbers of the ship creaked loudly and the waves lapped angrily against her sides. Father's head ached so badly that morning that he could only sit on the side of the bunk and hold it between his hands. With every roll and pitch of the ship, he moaned softly and closed his eyes.

"Run on deck, Jamie, and see what makes this ship toss about so," Mother said as she clung to the trunk for support. "Your poor father will never be able to get any rest at this rate."

James opened the cabin door and staggered up the hatchway, with John following close on his heels. When they reached the deck, they braced themselves against the bulwarks and hung on to each other for dear life. All about them was a dark green world of heaving water. The ship bucked over the waves like a frightened colt they had once seen in Uncle Alex's pasture. The masts groaned under the strain of the sails. A wave sprayed over the bulwark, thoroughly drenching them.

" 'Tis a bad blow!" they heard one of the sailors call out.

Above the shrieking of the wind through the rigging came the captain's voice, bellowing to the helmsman. "Steady, Mr. Browning, hold to your course!"

The helmsman hunched over the wheel, the muscles tight in his face.

"Reef the sails!" the first mate shouted.

The boys held their breath as they watched the crew scuttling up the ratlines and struggling along the swaying footrope to the yardarm where they perched precariously to reef in the cumbersome sails. Clutching and clawing at the unruly half acre of billowing canvas, they struggled to get the wind out of it and pass the gaskets around the yard beam. And none too soon, for the waves boiled white and the wind came again in a clap.

The ship wallowed and rolled, pitched and fell away in a most sickening manner. When a sudden gust struck her almost broadside, the boys could no longer cling to each other. They lost their balance and rolled across the slanting deck until they felt strong hands grasp their collars and drag them along the wet deck like sacks of potatoes. A burly seaman with a wet, grizzled beard opened a hatch and pushed them down the ladder. Drenched through and shivering with cold, they landed at the feet of the cook in the galley.

"Well, look what t'gale blew in!" cried the angry cook. "Don't ye land lubbers know enough to stow yerselves below deck when there's a blow?"

He helped them to their feet, gave them each a mug of hot soup, and let them warm themselves by the fire before they went back to their cabin. But before they left the galley, he gave them stern orders to stay below until the gale blew itself out.

A sudden gust struck the ship almost broadside. The boys lost their balance and rolled across the slanting deck.

When they returned to the cabin, Father was lying on the bunk and Mother was placing a damp towel on his forehead. She looked up at the boys with concern in her eyes.

"There's a storm at sea," John told her, his voice high with excitement. "It's awful up on the deck."

"The cook told us to stay in our cabin until it blows itself out," James added. "Is Father much worse?"

"Aye, he seems to have a fever," Mother told them. "If this ship would only quiet down!"

"I'll be all right, Mary," Father said, taking the wet towel from his forehead and trying to sit up. His eyes were red-rimmed and his face was flushed with fever. He swung his long legs over the side of the bunk and tried to stand, but he fell back with a groan.

"Help me up a wee bit, lads," he whispered hoarsely. "I'll not lie abed like this."

But Mother put her hand gently on his shoulder. "No, James. You must lie still and rest. Tomorrow you'll feel better."

But the next day Father was worse. He tossed in his bunk like the ship that was still tossing in the gale. His eyes were glassy and his body was burning with fever. Mother was so worried that she asked the boys to get the ship's doctor.

"No, no," Father protested through dry, cracked lips. "I'll be all right."

But Mother insisted that the boys find the doctor. "Go to the galley and ask the cook where he might be found," she told them.

Glad to leave the tiny cabin where there was nothing to do but watch their father's suffering, the boys fled to the galley. When the cook heard their story, he told them that Dr. McClure was somewhere in the steerage doctoring passengers who had become seasick because of the storm. The cook gave John a cup of warm herb tea and barley water, and while James went for the doctor, John took the tea to his father.

It smelled horrid and must taste as bad, John thought as he watched his father try to swallow the bitter mixture. At last James arrived with the doctor whose white wig was askew and whose face looked weary from being up all night with his patients.

Dr. McClure examined Father and told Mother that he had "ship's fever." He bled Father, and Mother tried to get him to eat. But all Father wanted was water and more water, and the boys were kept busy going back and forth from the cabin to the water breaker on the forward deck.

Although the wind had let up a bit the third day, the storm still raged, and with the continuing storm, their father's fever became worse. For several days he was delirious. Once when he floated to the surface of delirium, he sat up in his bunk, haggard looking, and wildly called for Jamie to take him to his loom.

The boys were so worried and frightened that they crouched close together on the top bunk and stared down in horror at the strange tormented creature their father had become.

By the end of the week the delirium passed, but it was just as hard to look at the pale, gaunt figure lying so still on the lower bunk and realize that this was once the strong, robust man who had never known a sick day in his life.

One night when another squall sent the wind

screaming in the rigging and the ship groaning and heaving again, their father called out to them. James heard Mother stirring below. He rolled over in the bunk and aroused John out of a troubled sleep.

"Johnny! Wake up! Father is calling our names!"

John's eyes opened wide and he scrambled down the bunk ladder after his brother. They knelt beside their father's bunk. Mother held the tin cup to Father's lips and he sipped a little water. The swinging candle-lantern that hung from a beam showed his eyes shining like black coals from his pale, hollow face. His cold, bony hands grasped theirs.

"Mary," he said, "open the Bible and read the Twenty-third Psalm."

"Oh, James!" Mother said in a choked voice.

"Aye, Mary, it's time to read it," Father said.

James brought the heavy family Bible from the trunk and Mother opened it.

" 'The Lord is my shepherd; I shall not want,' " she began. She tried to keep her voice steady but it trembled as she read, " 'Yea, though I walk through the valley of the shadow of death, I will fear no evil; for thou art with me; thy rod and thy staff they comfort me.' "

When she finished reading, Father spoke to them, his breath harsh and uneven. "Take good care of each other," he told them. "You will have to go on without me, but promise me that you will go to the Ohio Valley, where you can make a good home for yourselves."

A cough rattled in his chest. He closed his eyes and his voice was but a whisper. "A home where you can live in peace with your neighbors—"

His voice drifted off and his breathing came harder and slower and slower, and then it ceased. His hands relaxed and felt strangely heavy in theirs.

James knew that his father had died. The pain and the suffering were over and there was a strange look of peace on the thin, white face—a peace unlike any other that the boy had ever seen on his father's face before.

LAND HO!

IT seemed to James that his father's illness and the storm at sea were one and the same thing. Father had come down with the fever when the storm had begun and at his death the gale had finally blown itself out.

After the burial at sea, Mother spent much of her time alone in their cabin. Her gay, lighthearted laughter was muted now and her pretty blue eyes were filled with sadness. She spoke and ate very little. With their father's passing, all the joy and excitement of the voyage had vanished and time dragged heavily for the unhappy family.

Now that the ship rode easily on a calm sea, the boys stayed on deck most of the time. Sad and lonely, they spent their idle moments watching the ocean, but all they saw for days and days was an empty circle of gray-green water edging the far horizon.

To while away the time, they ran errands for the sailors or helped with some of the easier chores. They had taken a fancy to one seaman in particular named Sam Rawlings. Sam's weather-beaten face, as brown as mahogany, was like worn leather and a lock of straw-colored hair that fell across his forehead blazed out in contrast. Since their father's death Sam had been especially kind to them, cheerfully answering their questions about the ship. During the dogwatch, he told them tales of all the strange lands he had seen. Sam had sailed to many countries, but his favorite one was America.

"Methinks 'twill be a great country someday," he predicted as he sat with them on deck and spliced a piece of rope. " 'Tis big and growin' fast."

"Before our father died, he made us promise that we would go on to the Ohio Valley to make our new home," James said soberly.

Sam Rawlings lifted his brown face and squinted across the water. "Aye, mates, there's a whole big country out there. There be mountains and natural green meadows and brown prairies and deserts, all waiting to be settled by folks like ye."

Through Sam's eyes the boys saw this growing young America as their father had seen it, a land of freedom and opportunity.

One day Sam pointed to a sea gull flying above the bowsprit. "That be a sign we're nearin' land, mates," he exclaimed happily. "It won't be long now before the watch on the lookout sights land."

When shore birds were sighted the next day, the boys were so excited that they stayed on deck, even after dark, to search the dim horizon for land. The full moon rose and silvered the top of the mainmast, shining its pale light on the billowing sails; and in its brightness the boys kept watching the dark, empty sea. But it wasn't until the next morning that they heard the lookout shout, "Land ho!"

There was a rush of feet across the deck as sailors hurried up from the forecastle and passengers tumbled up from the cabins. "Let's get Mother," John shouted and the boys hurried toward the steerage to tell their mother the exciting news.

Mother followed them onto deck and they stood by the crowded rail on the portside while Sam pointed to a thin gray line on the western horizon.

"It looks to me like a cloud bank in the west," Mother said.

"Aye, but 'tis land, mum," Sam assured her. "Keep a weather eye on it and ye'll see 'tis land all right." He left them and hurried back to his duties.

Filled with excitement at their first glimpse of this new land, they kept their eyes on the gray line on the horizon until they could make out the white edge of breakers on a sandy beach and the trees and hills beyond. One of the passengers pointed to the mouth of a wide bay and told them that it must be Delaware Bay and when they sailed up the Delaware River, they would be in the city of Philadelphia.

Noisy sea birds dipped and wheeled all around them, calling out harsh notes of greeting, as they entered the bay. The boys looked excitedly at the forests which covered the banks of the wide river. It was now early May and the leaves on the trees were a new pale green. Pure white petals of dogwood brightened the dark pine barrens beyond.

"Look, Mother," John cried suddenly, "there's a house!"

"The first house we've seen in five weeks," exclaimed Mother, and for the first time since Father's death, a smile curved her lips and her blue eyes shone.

It was late afternoon when they approached the city of Philadelphia. Now they could see church spires pointing to the sky and the steep roofs of brick houses. Docks and warehouses lined the river's edge where ships flying flags from many countries lined the wharves.

"There be Christ Church steeple," said a familiar voice behind them. Sam Rawlings had joined them again at the rail. " 'Tis the tallest building in all America. It has eight bells in its tower, it has!"

He pointed to another tower. "An' that be the Pennsylvania State House where the Declaration of Independence was signed. See its square tower on the other side of town? Well, in that tower hangs the famous bell, Old Independence, which rang out freedom for America twenty-three years ago. Philadelphia is the largest city in the United States."

More passengers crowded on deck now, and the captain and officers were busy shouting orders to the crew. The boys gazed at the sloops and schooners they passed, riding at anchor on the dark waters by the piers. When they reached their own dock and the gangplank was down, the captain shouted, "All ashore! All ashore!"

"I'll help ye with your trunk, mum," offered Sam.

"Thank you, Mr. Rawlings," Mother replied. She stood bewildered, wondering what to do next. "I don't know where we'll stay. We don't know a soul in Philadelphia."

Sam Rawlings stroked his chin reflectively. "There be a snug little tavern on Water Street," he said. "As soon as I get shore leave, I'll take ye to it."

Mother thanked him gratefully, then they went into their cabin to pack the few things they had with them. As soon as Sam got leave, they were ready. With the boys' help, he carried their heavy trunk down the gangplank and onto the dock. Before they turned down the cobblestone street, Mother glanced back at the ship, at her tall masts, her spiderweb of rigging, and her billowing sails. There was sorrow on her face as she did so. It was as if she were saying a silent good-bye to Father for the last time.

"Come along," Sam said and they followed after him along the busy docks, around carts and bales, and through great crowds of people. "Keep a weather eye open for a sign readin' The Ship's Anchor," he told them. "That'll be the place I remember. 'Tis a small tavern but snug and shipshape, and t' owner is a good man and generous."

They hurried along Water Street, past brigs and schooners and clippers that thrust their proud bowsprits toward the tiny shops that lined the way. Eagerly the boys watched the tavern signs swinging back and forth in the breeze—The Tankard, The Jolly Roger, The Seafarer. It was Sam who spotted The Ship's Anchor first.

"There it be," he said, nodding ahead at a small red brick tavern, its sign creaking faintly above the door.

They set the chest down and Sam went inside to inquire about rooms. When he returned, he had a smile on his face.

"Ye be in luck, mum," he told Mother. "There be two rooms left. The tavern is no longer owned by the man I remember. The new owner is out of town but his wife seems all right and is willin' to put ye up. Come along now, mates. Help me take this old sea chest up to your rooms."

They entered a large low room dimly lighted by a three-pronged candlestick. The floor was cleanly sanded and crisp red curtains set off the windows. Several seafaring men were sitting at a table by the hearth, laughing and talking noisily. Above the mantel-shelf hung an old ship's anchor.

Mrs. Jenkins, the owner's wife, was a cheerful, wiry, little woman. With her dull brown hair, and dressed in a gray homespun dress and a frilly white mobcap, she reminded James of a small gray mouse. She greeted them with a smile and said in an apologetic tone as she led the way up a dark winding stairs, "I hope you won't mind being on the third floor. The two rooms up there are the only ones I have vacant. They are small but comfortable. I'll bring your supper to your rooms, if you like."

"Thank you," Mother said. "We are very tired."

After Mrs. Jenkins had left, Mother turned to Sam Rawlings. "I don't know how we can pay you for your kindness, Mr. Rawlings," she said gratefully. "We could not have managed without your help."

"Ye don't owe me a farthin', mum," replied Sam, grinning. "These two lads ran enough errands for me on board ship to pay for my services."

He turned to the brothers. "Well, mates, I must be getting along now, but before I leave, I'd like ye to have this." He pulled a folding knife hinged to a bone handle from his pocket. " 'Tis a penknife," he told them, opening one of the folding blades. "This second blade has a pointed steel pick for takin' stones from the hoofs of horses. A sailor like me don't need such a knife, but ye might need it on your trip over the mountains to the Ohio Valley. Here, take it and remember old Sam Rawlings when ye use it."

And before the two delighted boys could say a proper thank you, the sailor gave them a smart salute and started for the door. "Me best wishes t'all o'ye," he called over his shoulder before disappearing down the stairway.

Mother sat on the bed and smiled, the dimples showing in her cheeks. "Why, that was nice of Mr. Rawlings to give you such a fine knife," she said. "If all the folks we meet here in America are half as nice as he, we shan't have any worries."

While she began to unpack the trunk, the boys took Sam's gift to the window where they could see it better. They took turns opening and closing the blades.

At last they laid the knife on the little table by the bed and hurried across the hall to survey their own room. It was a small room, like Mother's, with a bed, a table, and a chair. A candle stood on the mantelshelf and a small fire burned on the grate. They walked over to the one window and were delighted to discover that it looked out on the street below where they could see the docks, the sailing ships, and the entire waterfront.

"Down there somewhere is Sam Rawlings," John said.

"Aye," replied James. "I hope we'll see him some-time again."

Mrs. Jenkins brought them a hot meal of roast beef and potatoes. As they began to eat, John declared, "This is the best meal I've eaten since we left Ireland."

"It does taste much better than the salt pork and sea biscuits we had on the ship," Mother agreed.

Her appetite seemed to have returned and with it there was a new determination in her voice. After they had eaten, she drew them to her side and said, "We must start to make plans. Tomorrow I'll ask Mrs. Jenkins how we can find a way to Pittsburgh, where we can inquire about Malcolm McPherson. That's what your dear father wanted and what we promised him we would do."

"A home where we can live in peace with our neighbors," John murmured, remembering his father's last words.

"But do we have enough money to get to Pitts-burgh, Mother?" asked the practical James.

Mary Graham shook her head. "No, I fear what we have left would not take the three of us to Pittsburgh, but I can sell the silver spoons. They will bring a good price. Tomorrow I'll ask Mrs. Jenkins where I can sell them."

"But Mother," James protested. "You can't sell your silver spoons!"

"You often said in Ireland you'd never part with them," John reminded her.

Mother nodded sadly. "Aye, the spoons have been in our family for generations, and I know I often said in Ireland that I would never part with them. But we aren't in Ireland now, my sons. We are in America and we need the money to travel to the Ohio Valley. I think what your father wanted us to do is more important than the spoons."

The boys had to agree, but the next morning when Mother brought Mrs. Jenkins to their rooms to show her the spoons, they felt downhearted with the thought of having to part with them.

"These are six of the King's silver spoons and they are very valuable," Mother told Mrs. Jenkins. "They've been in my family for many generations and I'm grieved to have to sell them. But it seems to be the only way."

Mrs. Jenkins picked up one of the spoons and held it gently in her hand.

"Such elegant silver," she murmured. "I, too, would feel sad to part with them." She sighed and nodded with understanding. "I remember the china dishes I brought from England when I was a young lass and came to America. They were my only remembrance from home and when I'd feel homesick for the old sod, I'd look at them for comfort. But when I married, I, too, had to sell them."

She placed the spoon with the others and stood a long moment looking thoughtfully at Mother and the boys. Suddenly her gray eyes brightened. "I have an idea," she told Mother. "If you have enough money for yourself, perhaps I can find you a ride on a wagon train going west. Then you can see about your land and the lads can stay here with me until you find a way to send for them. That way you can keep the spoons."

She smiled at James and John. "I could use two big boys who would be willing to work for their keep. It's not easy to get willing hands to work at a tavern when there's more money to be made elsewhere in the city."

Mother looked shocked at the idea and shook her head firmly. "I will never leave without my sons," she declared. "We will sell the spoons for money to buy a horse and wagon and will all go together."

Mrs. Jenkins frowned disapprovingly at what Mother had said. "There are many mountains to cross between here and the Ohio Valley. 'Twould be a hard trip over those mountains for a lone woman and two boys. And a dangerous one, too. The roads are steep and rocky. What if your wagon should break down? Many's the family that came back because they couldn't make it alone. 'Twould be a terrible risk."

"But how else can we get to the Ohio Valley?" asked Mother.

"Supply wagons head for Pittsburgh every week," Mrs. Jenkins replied. "I heard of a wagon train leaving by the end of this week. I can find out if they have room for another passenger. And later, when you can see yourself clear to send for the boys, I'll see that they get a ride across the mountains, too."

Again Mother shook her head and turned away.

"But Mother," James spoke up bravely, "we'll be all right here with Mrs. Jenkins until you can send for us."

"I promise the lads will have a good home with me," Mrs. Jenkins assured Mother. "With my husband gone to Virginia for supplies—and no telling when he'll be back—the boys will be doing me a favor, staying here and helping out at the tavern. The work will not be hard. 'Twill be caring for the stock and helping in the kitchen and such small chores."

"And we can keep the silver spoons!" urged John.

Mother pressed her fingers against her forehead and

37

closed her eyes. "I must have time to think about it," she said slowly.

Mrs. Jenkins nodded with understanding and stepped toward the door. "While you're making up your mind, I'll see if you can go with the wagon train. Now I must be about my chores." And she scurried from the room like a quick gray mouse.

Mother looked down at the silver spoons in her lap. She was quiet and thoughtful for a long time.

"Mrs. Jenkins is a kind lady, Mother," James said, sitting on the floor by her feet and putting his hand on her knee. "I like her."

"So do I," echoed John stoutly. "Besides, Jamie and I will be together."

"Aye, that's true," Mother said slowly, turning the thought over in her mind. "I suppose I could go on to Pittsburgh to find Malcolm McPherson and see about our land. Maybe he could lend me the money to send for you, and if not, perhaps I could find work in Pittsburgh to earn enough for your fare over the mountains."

"Then you will go?" asked John eagerly.

Mother looked up with a little frown between her eyes. "We will wait and see," she told them.

She put the spoons away in the trunk and for the rest of the day nothing more was said about how they would get over the mountains to Pittsburgh.

AT THE SHIP'S ANCHOR

THAT EVENING at supper Mrs. Jenkins brought news of the wagon train. It was leaving the day after tomorrow and the money Mother had would be enough for one fare. If she decided to go, one of the smaller wagons would come by the tavern for her.

At last Mother gave in to the boys' insistence that she go without them. "Pray God, I am doing the right thing," she told them. "If I didn't believe that Mrs. Jenkins is a kind and understanding woman and that I will be leaving you in good hands, I couldn't do this."

She cupped her hands around the chins of her sons and there was concern in her blue eyes. "Promise to take good care of each other. You must be good lads and do your chores faithfully. I will remember you both in my prayers each night."

"And we will remember you in ours," said John.

Mother packed her belongings in the big trunk, but she did not pack the silver spoons. Instead, she handed them to James.

"You are the man of the family now, son," she told him. "I want you to keep these spoons. If, for some reason, I cannot get the money to send you, then you must sell them for your fare to Pittsburgh. Mrs. Jenkins will help you get a ride on a wagon going west."

"But Mother!" James protested.

Mother shook her head and looked away. "Do as I say, James. Hide them under your mattress and keep them safely."

James did as his mother told him and tucked the linen bundle under his feather tick. When he returned to Mother's room, he found her sitting back in her chair with a quiet look on her face as if, now that her decision was made, a great burden had been lifted from her shoulders.

She looked up brightly and said, "It's such a pleasant day. Let's take a little walk. We haven't really seen Philadelphia yet."

The boys were glad to leave the little attic rooms and explore the city. Before they left the tavern, Mrs. Jenkins told them that all the streets crisscrossed like a checkerboard so that it would be easy to find their way.

"Let's walk to the State House where the famous bell, Old Independence, hangs in the tower," James suggested as he led the way down Water Street.

Mother smiled at her quiet, serious son. How straight and proud he walked, already assuming the role of the man of the family.

They gazed into shop windows where exotic merchandise from distant lands was displayed—tea from China, coconuts from the far Pacific, ivory from Africa, and bananas from the West Indies. They passed sailors mending sails and fishermen mending nets. In a vacant sea loft near the wharf they paused to watch a craftsman work on a figurehead for a ship's bow. They watched him shape the block of wood with mallet and chisel. The figurehead was the head of a beautiful woman, perhaps the shipowner's daughter.

At High Street they held their noses as they passed the fish market. Here the cobbled streets were littered with garbage and Mother gathered her skirts about her as they walked along. They were glad when they left the fish market behind them and came to Chestnut Street.

"Mrs. Jenkins said the State House is six squares up this street," James informed them.

As they walked west along the pleasant street, it seemed as if they were in a different world. Fine ladies with powdered hair passed them in chaises, and gentlemen in velvet coats and ruffled shirts clattered by on horseback. Somber Quakers in plain brown suits walked up and down the footways. Busy housemaids were scrubbing the marble steps on the white stoops in front of the fine brick houses.

"Philadelphia is a pretty city," Mother remarked as they walked under the large shade trees that lined the street.

When they reached Fifth Street, they stopped to

look at the stately Pennsylvania State House with its connecting piazzas and brick wings on either side. Their eyes followed the tall square tower to the belfry on top, and at that moment the great bell rang the hour. The boys held their breath as they listened to the round, full tones.

"That's the very bell that rang out independence for America twenty-three years ago," Mother said. "How strong and clear its tones are!"

The boys gaped in awe at the big bronze bell in the tower. "It has rung the noon hour," James said when the bell stopped ringing and its twelve deep tones echoed over the city.

"Aye, and we must be starting back," Mother told them.

"Let me lead the way," begged John. "I think I can find our way back to The Ship's Anchor."

Willingly, James let his brother take the lead. Now instead of being concerned about street signs, he could look about him at the sights of the city as they walked along. They passed the Custom House, Carpenters' Hall, and the bank. They passed the busy market place, where merchants shouted their wares and housemaids, with large market baskets hanging on their arms, bargained for the best price. At last they came to Front Street and glimpsed the river at the street's end.

John was pleased that he had brought them back to The Ship's Anchor without getting lost. "See, I know my way around the city," he told Mother proudly.

"Even so, you must never wander off alone, John," Mother warned. "Wherever you go, you must take James with you. You boys must always stay together."

The rest of that day and the next passed too quickly. At last it was time for Mother to leave them. Early in the morning a wagon stopped in front of The Ship's Anchor and the driver carried the big leather trunk to the back of the wagon and helped Mother onto a wooden seat behind him. There were three other passengers, a man and his wife and their young daughter.

Mother leaned over to kiss the boys good-bye. "Mrs. Jenkins said there is a post rider who carries mail between Pittsburgh and Philadelphia. I'll send a letter with the traveling money as soon as I can send for you."

The driver climbed up to his seat and clucked to his horses. "Good-bye, my sons, until we meet again," Mother said softly, her eyes brimming with tears. "May God grant that it will be soon."

James and John waved good-bye and Mother waved back until the wagon turned a corner and they could see her no more. Her long journey over the mountains to Pittsburgh had begun.

They turned and followed Mrs. Jenkins into the tavern. "We'll keep busy today, then we won't miss your mother so much," she told them. "James, lad, draw some water. 'Tis washday and I'll need many buckets to fill that iron cauldron. John, there's the hen house alongside the shed where we keep the cow. Maybe you'd like to hunt for eggs."

The boys went about their tasks willingly. Some of the lonesomeness for Mother left James as he got busy and drew water from the well in the garden. And John soon found himself whistling as he searched the nests in the hen house for eggs.

The boys worked hard and after each chore, Mrs. Jenkins praised them enthusiastically.

"I don't know how I managed before you boys came!" she exclaimed with delight.

Throughout the day the boys kept asking her for more things to do to keep them busy. Finally Mrs. Jenkins sank down in her rocking chair in the kitchen and said, "You plumb wore me out, thinking up things for you to do all day. We've done a week's work in one day. Now what's there to do tomorrow?"

The boys laughed with her and sat by the kitchen hearth while she told them stories of her girlhood days in England. Her father was a real gentleman, and they lived in a fine stone house in London. But she fell in love with a sailor—much too young she was then to know her own mind—and here she was in America. Yes, Mr. Jenkins sailed the seas until he lost a leg from a fall from the ship's rigging. It was then that they bought The Ship's Anchor with her inheritance and settled down in Philadelphia.

As the days went by, the boys kept busy with their chores. John fed the chickens and ducks with piggins of grain. He gathered eggs and milked the cow. He liked his work. It was like the chores he used to do for Uncle Alex when he visited the little farm in Ireland.

James carried wood and hauled buckets of water from the well. He helped Mrs. Jenkins in her vegetable garden. But the chore he liked best of all was waiting on tables in the common dining room during the night meal.

Whenever a ship came to port, the tavern was filled with noisy sailors, swaggering into the common room with their tarred pigtails, their swaying gold earrings, and their wide flopping blue pants.

"And spenders!" Mrs. Jenkins would say as she dished out the food for the boys to serve. "They toss their pieces of eight and guineas around as if they have a treasure chest full of coins back on the ship!"

The nights were always merry when sailors filled the tavern and the common room rang with cheerful noise. Like as not someone would play a mouth organ or a jew's harp and everyone would sing lustily around the big cheerful hearth. The boys soon learned the favorite sea chanteys and sang along with the seafaring men. Sometimes a mahogany-faced sailor came to the tavern with a green parrot from the tropics perched on his shoulder, and to the boys' delight the saucy bird would raucously mimick the sailors in their songs.

The summer passed quickly and pleasantly. Then one stormy day when the first flakes of snow swirled in the cold November air, a big man with a wooden leg and a seabag slung over his shoulder hobbled into the tavern. He wore an old sea jacket and a tattered felt tricorn hat. He had a large, red face, lightly marked by the pox, and a lantern jaw. A sullen expression tortured his mouth and his black eyes seemed to bore into the two brothers standing by the hearth. In a voice as loud as a cannon, he roared, "Wot's this, Mrs. Jenkins? Who be these two waifs?"

"Dan!" called his wife, hurrying from the kitchen and wiping her hands on her apron. "You've come home!"

"Aye, I be home," Mr. Jenkins replied gruffly. He let the seabag slip from his shoulder and scowled down at the boys.

"Now, then, who be these lads?"

In a quick, chirping voice, like a sparrow's, Mrs. Jenkins told the story of their poor father's death at sea, and of the journey their mother was making over the mountains to Pittsburgh. She ended by saying what good workers the boys were and how they were a great help to her at the tavern.

"Methinks they better be workin' good for their berth and victuals!" the landlord boomed. "Now step lively, woman, and bring me my dinner before I starve to death!"

So saying, he eased himself into one of the chairs and tossed his tricorn on the settle by the hearth.

Dismayed by their first impression of Mr. Jenkins, James and John hurried to fill his tankard and to place his dinner before him. After he ate, he went up to his room and slept for the rest of the day. In the evening he came down to the common room and assumed the role of the genial tavern keeper, slapping his old sea friends on their backs and filling their tankards with rum from the casks and bottles he had brought back from Virginia.

The men who came to The Ship's Anchor that night were different from the jolly sailors who had come to the tavern while the landlord was away. Long after the boys and Mrs. Jenkins had gone to bed, Mr. Jenkins and his friends drank and gambled in the common room. As James lay next to his brother and listened to the raucous song, drunken laughter, and cursing below, he wondered what their mother would say at such wicked goings-on.

"I'm glad she's not here now," he whispered to John as he pulled the pillow over his ears to shut out the loud noise. "If she knew, she'd never have agreed to let us stay here."

Life was quite different at The Ship's Anchor with Mr. Jenkins's return. The chores the boys had done so happily now became drudgery. There seemed to be no end of things the demanding landlord had them do. Split logs for the fire, haul water, run to the root cellar, feed the ducks and chickens, milk the cow, scrub and sand the floor, clean the fish. What next? And all the time, Mr. Jenkins never as much as lifted a hand to help. He sat by the fire, like a guest, smoking his long clay pipe or drinking from his tankard.

During the long dreary days of winter, the boys tried their best to please the surly landlord, but no matter how hard they worked, he never had a kind word for them and always managed to find more chores for them to do. They soon learned to keep out of his sight as much as possible.

When he was drunk from his own rum or was losing heavily in gambling with his friends he was at his worst. Then even Mrs. Jenkins kept as far away as possible from her husband.

One stormy day when John had forgotten to bring in enough wood for the fire, Mr. Jenkins gazed at him with bleary, wicked eyes. In his ugly voice, he bellowed, "Ye lazy swine! I'll knock it outa ye, so I will!" And with that, he gave the boy a heavy clout on the side of the head so that John reeled and stumbled across the floor. Bracing himself against a table and holding his aching ear where the landlord had hit him, the boy shook his head until the room came into focus again.

Mr. Jenkins started after him but as quick as a

scared cat James sprang to his brother's side. "Stop that!" he shouted angrily. "My brother didn't mean to forget the wood. You've no right to hit him like that."

The angry landlord turned on James next, and if it weren't for Mrs. Jenkins stepping between them, James had no idea what would have happened to him.

"Now, Dan, sit down," she said, trying to calm her husband. "John will bring in more wood and James will help him. They'll bring in twice the load, I promise you."

Mr. Jenkins glared at James but lowered his fist. "Give me yer bloody lip again, boy, and ye be sprawled out on that floor, ye will be!" Then muttering under his breath, he growled, "Sassy fellow, a ruffian if I ever saw one!"

After he had stormed out of the room, Mrs. Jenkins shook her head sadly. " 'Tis a weary time when Mr. Jenkins is gambling at cards and losing. Come along. I'll help you fetch more wood—then upstairs with you, John lad. I'll be up with a hot poultice for your ear."

That night, his ear still throbbing painfully, John whimpered, "Why doesn't Mother send for us? It's been a long time since she left."

"Most likely it's taking her a long time to earn enough money for our fare to Pittsburgh. But don't fret," James said lightly, trying to comfort his brother. "When spring comes, we should get a letter."

"I can't wait until we leave this place," John said in a half-choked voice. "I hate that old Mr. Jenkins."

And even though Mother had told them never to hate anybody, James had to admit, "So so I!"

The boys thought the long gray days would never

end, but finally the cold and snow gave way to warm sunshine and new green buds on the trees. Each day now they waited for a letter from Mother. But spring brightened into summer and still there was no letter.

Had something happened so that Mother couldn't send for them, James worried. The thought made him feel more miserable and desperate than ever. It was over a year now since Mother had left them and he began to wonder if they should ask Mrs. Jenkins to sell the silver spoons as Mother would have wanted them to do if she couldn't send for them.

James worried about this all the way to the market one day. "Let's find out where the wagon trains leaves Philadelphia for Pittsburgh," he said to John after they had purchased the tobacco and cheese Mr. Jenkins had sent them for.

"Do you think we dare?" asked John, wide-eyed. "You know what Mr. Jenkins will do if we don't come right back."

"Aye," James muttered grimly, "he'd make us work that much harder. But come on. We don't get away from the tavern very often. Now's our chance to find out."

The cheese merchant told them that wagons went up High Street to the Schuylkill River, where they crossed over on the ferry. The boys thanked the merchant for his directions. They followed High Street west until they came to the river. In the shade of a great oak, they flung themselves down on the green riverbank to rest.

"Look, there's the ferry crossing the river now," John said, pointing to a large flatboat filled with horses and people.

They watched the ferry until it reached the far shore where they glimpsed farms and fields and a hazy mountain in the distance. Somewhere beyond that mountain was the western country and their mother, James thought, and more than ever he longed to be on their way to Pittsburgh.

John got to his feet and brushed the grass off his pants. "We better be getting back now."

James nodded reluctantly. With the market basket between them, they trudged back over the cobbled streets toward the waterfront.

When they returned to The Ship's Anchor, Mr. Jenkins had more chores waiting for them. For the rest of the long day it was work, work, work, such as the boys had never dreamed possible. They were almost too weary that night to climb the steps to their attic room. John stumbled into bed at once, but James stopped short and looked around the dim room. As tired as he was, he sensed that something was wrong.

He moved the tallow candle around and by its dim light saw that the room had been ransacked. The chair was overturned and their clothes were thrown off the wooden pegs along the wall. The quilt was torn off the bed.

John was sprawled out on the bare tick. "Get up!" James shook his brother. "Somebody's been in our room."

Wearily John rolled off the bed. Still half-asleep, he held the candle while James lifted the mattress. Frantically, the older boy searches under it for the linen bundle in which the six silver spoons were wrapped. But the spoons were not where he had hidden them.

Now wide-awake with worry, John held the light close to the bed while James searched a second time under every inch of the feather tick. When he finished, he slumped down on the bed and the brothers stared at one another with wide, frightened eyes. The spoons were gone!

ESCAPE IN THE NIGHT

FOR A FEW LONG MOMENTS they sat in the dark room, too upset to talk. Then James found his voice. There was a hollow ring to it as he reasoned, "While we were away today, someone must have ransacked our room and found the spoons."

"But who could it be?" asked John. "Nobody knew about Mother's spoons except Mrs. Jenkins and she wouldn't take them."

"It must have been Mr. Jenkins," James declared, his eyes darkened with anger. "Somehow he must have found out about them."

"Oh, Jamie, we have to get them back!" exclaimed John in a small, tight voice. "If we don't hear from

Mother, we'll have to sell the spoons to get to Pittsburgh."

Sick with worry and fear, James blinked hard in the darkness. Mother had said that he was the man of the family now and she had entrusted the spoons to his care. He should have guarded them day and night. He felt miserable that they were gone. He put his arm across his eyes to hold back the tears and tried to think what to do.

If Mr. Jenkins took the spoons, it wouldn't be long before he sold them—if he hadn't already—to pay his gambling debts. There was only one thing they could do now, James decided. They would have to tell Mrs. Jenkins about the missing spoons. She was the only one who could help them.

"Let's go downstairs and ask Mrs. Jenkins what to do, Johnny. She was in the kitchen washing out tankards when we came up to bed."

"Aye," the younger boy agreed, "and Mr. Jenkins was in the common room playing cards. If we slip down the back stairs, he won't see us."

They blew out the candle and made their way down the back stairway in the dark. At the bottom they opened the door to the kitchen a crack and peered through it. They were in luck. Only Mrs. Jenkins was there, filling the clean tankards for the thirsty guests in the common room. She almost dropped one when she heard the door squeak open and saw their two frightened faces staring out at her.

"Why, lads," she exclaimed, "I thought you had gone to bed!"

James left John at the door to the common room to keep an eye on Mr. Jenkins while he hurriedly told

Mrs. Jenkins about the missing spoons. The little woman frowned and twitched her lips as she listened. Then with a weary sigh she said, "Aye, it could have been Dan, though for all his faults he has never stolen before that I know of. But I do know he's run up a lot of gambling debts of late."

She paused for a moment, then in a voice barely above a whisper, she murmured what James had been asking himself over and over again. "How could Dan have known about your mother's spoons? I have never told him about them."

Her small face was pinched with worry at the thought. Then her gray eyes snapped and she said crisply, "You two best go back to your room. If Dan has taken those spoons, I think I know where they might be. Go along now and stay in your room, mind you. Don't leave it until you hear my knock." And with that she hurried them up the stairway and turned to take the tankards into the common room as if nothing had happened.

Back in the attic room the boys sat on the edge of the bed and waited in the darkness. They strained their ears to each sound in the night, to the echo of husky voices in the common room below, to the faint sound of a ship's bell on the river outside, to the pounding of their own hearts.

They listened and waited for what seemed like hours. Bone-tired and sick with worry, John wished he could just lie back on the bed and go to sleep, to wake in the morning and discover that this had been just a bad dream. He drew in a trembling breath and shifted uneasily on the bed. "Why doesn't she come?"

"We'll have to be patient," James whispered in a

hushed, anxious voice. "Probably she's hunting for the spoons."

They waited and listened. The night was sultry. Across their dark window lightning flickered on and off. The dull sound of thunder rumbled in the distance. Presently they heard the first drops of rain drumming on the roof above their heads.

Then they heard another sound—a soft knock on the door. James leaped up to open it. Like a frightened night creature, Mrs. Jenkins scurried into the room. She held a short candle in one hand. In the other was a large market basket with a white towel over it.

"I found the spoons," she said breathlessly after James quickly closed the door behind her. "They were in the old sea trunk in the cellar, as I thought they'd be. Dan always keeps his valuables there. I've hidden them in the bottom of this basket, under some food. Now, lads, this is my plan. You must leave the tavern tonight—as soon as we can get your things together. Mr. Jenkins is in the common room and losing badly again at cards. Tomorrow for sure he'd sell the spoons."

James hesitated. "But won't he be angry that you found them?"

The woman shook her head. "When he discovers you two have gone, he'll think you found them, no matter what I say. And he'll be after you for sure first thing in the morning. You must keep hidden the best way you can. There are many old buildings and dark alleys in the city where you can hide tonight. Tomorrow, as soon as you can, find a wagon going out of the city."

She pressed a few coins into James's hand. "Give the

driver these and tell him you are on your way to Pittsburgh to find your mother. Ask him to take you across the river on the ferry. Then wait there for a supply wagon going west. The silver spoons will be more than enough to pay your fare to Pittsburgh."

She hesitated a moment to catch her breath. When she spoke again her voice was gentle and sad. " 'Tis sorry, I am, that I couldn't sell the spoons for you and get you a ride to Pittsburgh myself. But there is no time for that now, lads. You must be off tonight."

With that, she handed James the basket. Scooping a blanket off the floor, she hurriedly gathered up their clothes and wrapped them in a bundle. Knotting the ends of the blanket together, she handed the bundle to John to carry.

"I'll slip down the back stairs first, and if the coast is clear I'll rap on the bottom stair three times," she told them. "Go out the back way and through the gate in the garden fence. Make your way toward the Schuylkill as fast as you can without being seen."

Before she left, she turned to kiss their cheeks tenderly. "You are good lads and I shall sorely miss you. I hope and pray that soon you'll be with your own dear mother again. And now good-bye." She kissed them hurriedly again before opening the door and slipping out into the dark hallway.

They listened breathlessly to her light footsteps on the back stairs and when they heard three soft knocks on the bottom step, they slipped down the dark way after her. She held the back door open for them.

"Godspeed!" she said softly. And with a fond, last look at the kind little woman, they slipped out into the night.

Like fleeting shadows they made their way past the well and barn and out through the back gate into a narrow, winding alley which led to Front Street. The shower had passed but dark clouds scudded across the sky, veiling a pale, watery moon.

James gave a last, fleeting glance back at the forest of masts and rigging along Water Street, rising against the night sky. Then he turned and looked ahead. The ship's bell grew fainter and soon the familiar sights and sounds of the waterfront disappeared into the night.

They hurried along past dark warehouses that seemed to frown down disapprovingly on the two stealthy boys, and past taverns that threw their light accusingly across their way from clouded bottle-glass panes. James felt as if each strange shadow they passed would turn into the angry landlord of The Ship's Anchor and that they would be dragged back to the tavern and beaten. He breathed a light sigh of relief when, at last, they had reached High Street.

Now they crept past the backs of fine brick homes and carriage houses, keeping to the shadowy alleys and away from inquisitive night watchmen. They were about to cross a main thoroughfare when, just in time, they spied the glow from a lantern coming toward them. They hid in the shadows and listened for the watchman's footsteps, not daring to venture across the street until they were sure he had turned the corner.

When he was well out of sight, they hurried across and ducked into a dark stable behind an inn. Too weary to run any farther, they climbed into the stable loft and sank down into the soft hay.

"Pray hard, Johnny," James whispered breathlessly.

"Pray hard that Mr. Jenkins doesn't find us here."

But exhausted, John was already sound asleep. James slid down against the pile of hay and sat huddled in the inky shadows of the loft. He let his head drop, only meaning to doze a little, but the last thing he heard before he sank into a deep sleep was the voice of the returning watchman crying out, "Eleven o'clock on a cloudy night and all's well!"

They were awakened the next morning by the sound of footsteps and the heavy *clop, clop* of horses' hoofs. They rubbed the sleep from their eyes and crept to the edge of the loft to peer down into the stable.

A stableboy was leading a team of two grays to a wagon in the innyard. The wagon was small but sturdy, with a canvas top. A man was busy loading a heavy cowhide trunk into the back.

He was a young man, lean and rawboned, like the tall Scotch-Irishmen the boys knew back in Ulster. He had dark, curly hair and wore a long black coat, black knee breeches, black stockings, and black buckled shoes.

When the stableboy had hitched the horses to the wagon, the man paid him and mounted the high wagon seat. He took up the reins then let them fall slack.

"Oh," he called out suddenly to the stableboy, "I forgot something. Hold the team, lad, while I go back to the inn and fetch my hat."

The stableboy turned his head toward the inn, waiting for the young man to come out. James hissed, "Come on! Let's sneak aboard the wagon."

58

The boy took hold of the lead rein while the young man nimbly climbed down from the wagon seat and made his way across the innyard. There was something about the way the man looked and the way he acted that made James trust him. He nudged John sharply with his elbow. "He's leaving the city. Did you see his trunk?"

"Aye." The younger boy nodded.

"Well, here's our chance for a ride," whispered James.

"Do you think he'll take us?" asked John anxiously.

James blinked his eyes. He hadn't thought about the possibility of the man's refusing. Should they wait until he came out of the inn and ask him? They had the coins Mrs. Jenkins gave them to pay him. But suppose for some reason the man refused to take them?

The thought of how angry Mr. Jenkins would be when he found the spoons missing flashed through James's troubled mind. They had to get out of the city fast, before the angry landlord found them. Here was a way out and there was little time left before the young man would return to the wagon. James made up his mind in a hurry.

"Follow me and be quiet, Johnny. We'll sneak aboard the wagon and he won't find us until we're out of the city. We'll pay him for the ride then."

They gathered up their belongings and quietly climbed down the loft ladder. Careful to keep out of sight of the stableboy, they edged their way stealthily to the door. When the stableboy turned his head toward the inn, waiting for the young man to come out, James hissed, "Come on!"

With their hearts pounding in their chests, the boys

slipped out of the stable and crept across the yard to the back of the wagon. They put their bundles into the wagon. Then James bent over to give John a boost up. No sooner had John landed in the wagon than one of the horses nickered and stamped as if he sensed the boys' presence.

The stableboy turned to quiet the horse and at that moment James's courage seemed to ebb right out of him. He flattened himself against the back of the wagon and held his breath.

"Whoa thar, now!" the stableboy called to the horse. "What ails ye?"

The horse quieted and when the boy turned his gaze back to the inn, John quickly leaned over the end of the wagon and helped pull his brother in. Like two fugitives they sat huddled together under the canvas top. Neither one moved nor spoke. At last they heard the man's footsteps and the squeak of the high wagon seat as he settled himself once more at the reins. They heard him call good-bye to the stableboy, then he clucked at the grays and the wheels started grating over the stones of the innyard.

The boys crouched farther back into the shadows of the wagon as they jounced along over the cobblestone street. Only once did they dare to take a peek out the canvas back.

A flood of relief surged over James when he saw the direction they were going. It was west on High Street and when he glimpsed the blue waters of the Schuylkill, he knew for sure they were leaving the city.

They kept well hidden while they crossed the river on the ferry. Not until they were on the other side did they straighten their stiff legs and relax.

61

A smile brightened James's face as he glanced through the opening in the canvas and watched the city growing smaller and smaller on the other side of the river. "We did it, Johnny," he whispered. "We're on our way and we're heading west!"

"Can we eat now?" John whispered back. "I'm starved."

James nodded and lifted the towel that covered the market basket. Under it the boys discovered a loaf of bread, a large wedge of cheese, some cold ham, and an apple pie that Mrs. Jenkins had packed for them. At the bottom of the basket was the precious linen bundle. James opened the cloth to make sure the silver spoons were really there, and when he saw them sparkling in the sunlight that filtered through the back of the wagon, he felt so happy he could have danced a jig right there on the wagon bed.

He quickly rewrapped the spoons in the linen and placed them back in the basket again, then stared with pleasure at all the food. There seemed to be enough to last them a week. As they ate some of the cheese and bread, memories of the little woman who had packed it flashed through James's mind. Never, as long as he lived, would he forget Mrs. Jenkins and her kindness.

Now that they had left the cobblestone streets behind them and the road was smooth and straight, the driver flicked his snake whip above the horses' heads, and the big grays trotted along at a good pace. The young man relaxed on the high wagon seat and began to sing. The tune was a familiar hymn the boys remembered in Ireland. The driver's deep, powerful voice sounded more like a choir than one man and his singing made John feel so lighthearted that if they hadn't been stowaways, he would have sung along with the merry driver.

There was much traffic on the road. They passed stagecoaches and carriages, farmers' wagons and little carts going to and from the city. Several times their driver had to stop his singing and pull the two grays to the edge of the road to make way for the enormous covered wagons carrying freight into the city.

The boys stared as these huge, strange-looking wagons rumbled by. With their blue wagon beds dipping down in the middle and their billowy white canvas tops blowing in the wind, they resembled ships on wheels. Hoops of bells, arched over the horses' collars, jingled merrily as they passed by.

As they traveled farther into the country, the traffic thinned and the boys were able to view the stone farmhouses, the cleared fields, the deep woods, and the pretty meadows that lined the road. Once they glimpsed a milestone pointing westward with the name "Lancaster" on it.

The sun at the back of the wagon climbed higher in the sky and when it was just overhead, the driver pulled his horses to the side of the road and stopped.

He leaped down from the wagon seat. With pounding hearts, the boys heard him coming to the back of the wagon. No longer could they hide themselves. Suddenly they were staring right into the driver's startled face.

For a long moment none of them said a word. James's stomach felt hollow as he looked into the intensely blue eyes that stared back at them under dark, frowning brows.

"Well, now, what have we here? Stowaways, is it?"

And although the man's voice was exclaiming, James thought, for a moment, he detected a twinkle in those flashing blue eyes.

He swallowed the lump in his throat and muttered, "Aye—sir."

"You're not bound boys, thinking of running away now, are you?" the driver asked quickly.

John's startled eyes were round and innocent. "Oh, no sir!"

The young man looked puzzled and a bit doubtful, but he said. "Well, I'll tell you what we'll do. We'll go to that little stream over yonder and have something to eat. Then I'll hear your story."

The boys scrambled down from the back of the wagon, and the driver brought out a small sack and set it on a flat rock near the stream.

"This is what the cook at the inn packed for my lunch," he said, opening the sack. "I fear it's not much but we can divide what there is."

"Oh, we have our own lunch," John spoke up quickly, and he ran back to the wagon for their basket of food.

When the young man saw all the food Mrs. Jenkins had packed, he threw back his head and laughed. "And I was worried that we wouldn't have enough to eat! I should have remember that the Lord always provides. Now let's give Him thanks."

They bowed their heads and in a deep, solemn voice the young man gave thanks to God for the food before them and asked Him to guide them on their way and to give them courage of soul and strength of body for the journey ahead.

When he finished the prayer, John said curiously,

"You pray like our Pastor McCosh back in County Antrim."

"Well, now, I am a preacher," the man told them. "My name's Thomas Murray, but most folks call me Mr. Tom. I travel the back roads to bring the gospel to settlements where there are no churches. I'm what folks call a circuit rider."

"How far west are you going, sir?" James asked curiously.

"To Pittsburgh," Mr. Tom replied. "I came to Philadelphia for a trunkload of Bibles and hymnbooks for folks in the back country who haven't got them."

The boys looked at the circuit rider with surprise. "You mean you'll be going all the way to Pittsburgh!" exclaimed John.

"That's where my home is," the man replied. "When I'm not riding the circuit, I live with my older sister and her family. Now, what about you two? What are your names and where are you headed?"

While they divided their lunches and ate, James, with John chiming in now and then, told the circuit rider their names and their long story from the day they left Ireland until they had slipped into his wagon in Philadelphia.

James reached into the bottom of the basket and drew out the silver spoons. "If you take us with you to Pittsburgh, sir, we can pay for our way with these spoons."

Mr. Tom bent over to examine them. "They are quite valuable, I see."

"Yes, sir. They have been in our family for a long time."

"Wrap them up, lad, and keep them with you

safely. I could not take such valuable heirlooms. They belong with your family and should always stay there."

A shadow crept across John's face. "Then you won't take us to Pittsburgh?"

"I didn't say that, lad. I'll be glad for your company on my long journey. Now that you're here and there's no way back, you're welcome to come. But I cannot accept your spoons."

"We do have a few coins that Mrs. Jenkins gave us," James spoke up quickly, digging deep into his coat pocket for the money.

"No, no, lad. I cannot take your money nor your spoons. You and your brother can pay for your journey by helping me along the way. But I must warn you, it will be a long, hard ride over the mountains to Pittsburgh. It will take a lot of courage to get there."

"Oh, we'll work hard," John offered eagerly.

"And we have the courage to get there," James added stoutly.

The circuit rider rose to his feet and clapped a hand on their shoulders. "I believe you have," he told them.

"Then we *can* come with you—all the way to Pittsburgh?" asked James, hardly daring to believe their good fortune.

The circuit rider smiled down at the two eager faces that peered expectantly into his own. "That you can, lads," he answered merrily. "That you can!"

MR. TOM

BEFORE they started out again, the circuit rider watered the horses and examined their feet to see that there were no sharp stones caught in the bottom of their shoes.

"A horse can go lame that way," he told John, who was standing by watching.

The boy's eyes shone approvingly as he watched the circuit rider gently lift one hoof after another and talk to the horses as he did so. Mr. Tom handled his big grays with as much love and care as Uncle Alex had handled Old Angus.

"Been around horses all my life," Mr. Tom said. "One thing a circuit rider has to be besides a good

67

preacher and that's a good horseman."

He laid a hand on the withers of the lead horse and his voice was full of praise. "This one is Joshua. He's the horse I take with me when I ride the circuit. He's always willing to carry me along the hard roads of the back country. And his partner here is Job, a good and patient follower."

As John rubbed down Joshua's pastern, he remembered the folding knife Sam Rawlings had given them. James said he could carry it because he had taken such a fancy to it. John plunged his hand into his pocket and brought it out now. He opened the steel pick for taking stones from horses' hoofs and showed it to Mr. Tom.

The circuit rider examined the blade with interest. "It'll come in mighty handy on this trip and save us hunting for sharp sticks along the way."

John smiled, pleased with what Mr. Tom had said about the knife. He put it carefully back in his pocket and helped tighten up the harness.

When they were ready to leave, Mr. Tom said, "How about you boys riding on the seat with me. You can see the road much better up here."

The boys climbed up over the big front wheel. Then Mr. Tom flicked the snake whip over the horses' heads and they were off once more.

Ahead the road stretched broad and smooth and Mr. Tom sang one hymn after another. They passed prosperous-looking farms with sturdy barns and houses built of gray fieldstone. The boys had never seen such beautiful farmland. The fields were large and rolling and the orchards along the way were heavy with fruit.

Mr. Tom interrupted his hymn singing to tell them

that they were passing through the land of the Amish and the Mennonites. "These industrious people came to America from Switzerland and Germany so that they could live in peace and be free to worship God in their own way."

"Like us Ulstermen," James piped up proudly. "We came to America for the same reasons."

"Yes, you did," Mr. Tom replied.

Several Amish families, riding in black, boxlike wagons, passed them on the road. The men wore black suits and broad-brimmed black hats. The women wore blue dresses with black aprons and black sunbonnets. The children had rosy red cheeks and smiled shyly when Mr. Tom waved to them.

Suddenly John shouted, "Look, here comes another one of those big wagons! See—around that bend in the road."

Mr. Tom pulled the team to the side of the road as a large freight wagon swung around the bend up ahead. What a sight it was with its blue sides, its red wheels, and its billowy white canvas top!

"We never saw such big covered wagons in Ireland," James remarked.

"They're Conestoga wagons," answered Mr. Tom. "They're called that because they are built in the Conestoga Valley here in Pennsylvania. See how the wagon bed dips down in the middle and tips up in the front and back? Well, they're built that way so that when they go up and down steep mountain roads, the freight won't fall out the ends. Those wagons are helping America grow by carrying people and freight from the east to the west."

"Do you suppose Mother traveled to Pittsburgh in a

wagon like that?" John asked.

"She probably did," Mr. Tom replied.

John continued, his eyes sparkling, "I'd like to be a driver on one of those Conestoga wagons someday."

"Well, the Lord willing, maybe someday you will," replied Mr. Tom, "but you'll have to do some growing first. Did you notice how big and strong that driver was?"

John nodded. "Aye, when we find Mother and I eat her good cooking again, I'll start growing!"

Mr. Tom chuckled and John laughed back. He was glad they were going to Pittsburgh with the jolly circuit rider. He liked the way Mr. Tom talked and sang and the way he laughed. And he sure knew how to handle horses.

Later in the afternoon Mr. Tom let John hold the reins, and by the time they stopped for the night, the boy felt as if he were a seasoned driver. He helped unhitch the grays and rub them down while James unfastened the feed trough under the back of the wagon and placed it along the wagon tongue. Mr. Tom filled it with grain he had brought from Philadelphia. While the horses were munching contentedly, he took his flint and steel and made a fire.

"This is as good a place as any to camp for the night," he told them, glancing around at the clump of sheltering trees and the small stream nearby. "I always try to camp along a stream and not too far back from the road. In the mountains, I sometimes stop at cabins or settlements along the way. Folks in the back country who have no churches hunger for the Word of God and are always glad to see me. When they know I'm coming, they gather together from miles around and we have a meeting. We sing and pray and I talk to them about the Lord. Sometimes I perform a wedding or preside at a funeral. It's the weddings I like best."

After they had eaten more of Mrs. Jenkins' good food, Mr. Tom brought out his Bible and read some verses before they rolled up in their blankets. He read about not worrying about their lives, what they had to eat or drink or what they had to wear, for as God fed the birds in the sky and clothed the lilies in the field, so He would feed and clothe them.

It was comforting to hear Mr. Tom's deep gentle voice read those words. For the first time in many nights the boys fell into a peaceful sleep, knowing that their long journey westward had begun and that God would take care of them.

They awoke next morning to the songs of birds and a beautiful clear day. After breakfast they started out on the road again. Their second day of traveling was much like the first. In the evening they made camp again by the roadside just outside the town of Lancaster.

When they rode into Lancaster the next day, Mr. Tom stopped at the marketplace to buy bread, fresh eggs, milk, meat, and coffee. The Mennonite farmer and his young son who sold them the provisions helped load them into the wagon. They ate their noonday meal on the wagon seat as they rode along, for Mr. Tom wanted to reach Chambers' Ferry by nightfall.

The sun was already dipping behind the trees on the western shore of the river when they finally reached the ferry. The Susquehanna was much larger than the little Schuylkill. It was so wide that in the middle of the river were several large islands covered with groves of trees.

As they waited their turn at the ferry, the boys looked over their fellow travelers. Some were on horseback and others rode in wagons like Mr. Tom's or led pack horses. A fine carriage and small farmers' carts were waiting at the landing to be carried across on the ferry.

When at last it was their turn, Mr. Tom drove his horses carefully onto the large flat ferry boat. John climbed down over the wheel to hold Joshua's bridle in case the big horse should become frightened and bolt. But as the men on the ferry pushed the boat across the river with their long poles, Joshua and Job not as much as flicked an eyelash.

When the bow touched the landing on the far side of the river, Mr. Tom drove the grays up the landing slope that led onto a narrow road along the riverbank. That night they camped with the other weary travelers on the western shore of the Susquehanna.

John awoke early the next morning. He sat up in his blanket and rubbed the sleep from his eyes. The sky in the east was pearl gray with a thin edge of pink along the horizon.

Some of the travelers were already up and moving about. John threw off his blanket and rose, shivering, to his feet. He started out on a run toward the grassy spot along the riverbank where the two grays had been hobbled during the night. He would surprise Mr. Tom and water the horses so that they could be hitched to the wagon.

But when he came to the place where they had been hobbled, he stopped short. The horses weren't there.

He peered all around him through the gray dawn. To his startled surprise, he spied the grays being led to the river by a tall man dressed in buckskins. John stood frozen. But only for a moment.

"Hey!" he called out as loudly as he could. "Come back with those horses!" And in the next breath he shouted, "Mr. Tom! Mr. Tom! Someone's stealing our horses!"

To his amazement the buckskin-clad figure stopped dead in his tracks and turned toward him. The next moment a laugh rang out in the quiet morning air. The horse thief turned out to be none other than Mr. Tom himself!

Instead of the familiar black coat, the circuit rider was wearing a fringed-caped hunting jacket that reached halfway down his thighs. A pair of deerskin leggings replaced the black knee breeches and he wore a pair of soft Indian moccasins instead of the black, buckled shoes. With a wide-brimmed straw hat cocked on the side of his head, he looked more like a woodsman or a trapper than a preacher.

The boy ran up to him and at his startled expression, Mr. Tom explained, "I always dress like this when I'm in the back country. It's much easier traveling the mountain roads dressed in my buckskins."

John eyed the long hunting knife and small ax that were tucked in the leather belt tied behind Mr. Tom's hunting shirt. A deerskin pouch and a wooden canteen were slung over one shoulder. John drew in a long, wistful breath. He'd give almost anything to have an outfit like that.

As they traveled westward that day, the boys soon learned what the circuit rider meant by the back country. After they left the little village of Carlisle behind them, the road westward became narrow and hilly. The farms along the way were more scattered and at times they rode miles without passing a house at all.

All day they kept following a mountain that loomed up ahead of them like the shaggy back of a great sulking beast. And the next day when they followed the road over the mountain, John wished more than ever that he had a buckskin suit and a pair of moccasins like Mr. Tom's.

Tree branches and thornbushes along the way tore at the boys' linsey-woolsey suits. When the road was steep and they had to climb off the wagon seat to walk alongside the horses, their feet ached in their stiff leather shoes.

That night as they sat around the campfire nursing sore feet, Mr. Tom brought out a medicine bottle from underneath the wagon seat. He uncorked it, and John wrinkled his nose as the circuit rider rubbed some of the oil on his feet.

"It smells terrible," he said.

"It's rattlesnake oil to heal the blisters," Mr. Tom explained. "Indians use it to toughen their feet so that they can climb up and down these rocky trails. When we get to Shawnee cabins, we'll trade some of our provisions for buckskins and moccasins for you boys."

After some of the foul-smelling oil was rubbed on James's feet, Mr. Tom put the bottle back in the wagon and sat down by the fire again. The boys enjoyed these nights around the campfire when the circuit rider told them stories about this new country. He had told them how America won her independence, just nineteen years ago, and that George Washington had been the new country's first President. Now there was a second President, John Adams, and the new nation was growing westward over the mountains.

"By settling in the Ohio Valley, you boys and your mother are helping America grow," Mr. Tom had said.

Tonight as they watched the flames dance in the campfire, Mr. Tom was telling them about life west of the Susquehanna River before America became a free nation. "There were no farms or villages here then," he said, "only forts that the English army built on their march across the mountains to the Ohio Valley. In fact the road we're taking over the mountains to Pittsburgh was a military road that connected those forts during the French and Indian War. It's called the Forbes Road and was named for General John Forbes, who built it."

When the campfire burned low and they had rolled up in their blankets, Mr. Tom said, "Keep your feet pointed close to the fire the way Indians and hunters do. The heat will help take away the soreness."

Wrapped snugly in his blanket, James looked up through the tree branches to the sky. At first it had seemed strange sleeping with his clothes on and not having a roof over his head. But now he was getting used to going to bed under the stars. He liked listening to the embers crack in the campfire and the katydids rasping their answering calls through the treetops. He watched a bat flutter and tilt above a flame that had leaped up from the glowing embers.

His feet had stopped throbbing and he felt warm and comfortable. He reached his hand into his jacket pocket where he now kept the precious linen bundle. He could feel the hard shape of the silver spoons through their cloth wrapping and it made him think of Mother somewhere far over these mountains.

His eyes flickered in the glow from the burning coals and before he knew it, he was dreaming of Mother and how surprised and pleased she was that they had saved her silver spoons.

TROUBLE ON SIDELING HILL

IT was a hot, humid day in August. The cicadas were singing their prolonged shrill notes in the tops of trees and the woods were thick with black flies that kept buzzing and stinging unmercifully. The air was heavy and still, and Mr. Tom predicted thundershowers before the day was over.

As they trudged up the mountain road, James thought how different this steep dark forest was from the open countryside and gently rising hills of Ireland. What he would give for just one breath of brisk, cool sea air again!

His brother's painful voice broke into his reverie. "I can't walk one step farther, Jamie," groaned John,

77

flopping down on a log beside the rocky road and kicking off his shoes which were full of holes.

James came quickly to his brother's side. "Oh, yes you can," he said in a determined voice. "Get up, Johnny. You remember what Mr. Tom said—that it would take courage to get over these mountains."

John struggled to his feet with a groan. "I don't know why they call this mountain a hill," he grumbled. "It's much steeper than the Tuscarora Mountains we crossed yesterday."

They looked ahead to where the circuit rider was leading Joshua and Job up the steep rise. It had been several days since they had left the wooded valleys of the East. They had gone through the little town of Shippensburg and had climbed through a pass in the Blue Mountain. After leaving Fort Littleton, they had ridden for awhile in the wagon. But now that they were climbing Sideling Hill, they had to walk so that the horses would have less to pull.

James wondered how the two grays could keep from sliding down the steep road. But the two faithful beasts kept straining at their collars and the wagon kept rumbling slowly upward.

The boys trudged on up the road, John automatically moving one weary foot in front of the other. The narrow, winding road kept rising ahead of them forever, it seemed, twisting steeply up, up the mountain. As they rounded a sharp turn, they glimpsed, in the deep, wooded gully below, the remains of a big

The circuit rider led the horses slowly down the steep grade. The boys slipped and slid over loose rocks and stumbled over stumps of trees.

Conestoga wagon that had gone off the road, its once blue sides broken and weathered gray. They wondered what had happened to the horses and the driver of that wagon.

They went on and on until, when James himself thought he could not take another step, they finally reached the summit. They sank down on a rocky outcropping from which the land dropped away on all sides. Below them the full sweep of land spread out like a sea of solid treetops that rolled on and on until its faint blue crests broke against the far western horizon.

Mr. Tom stood looking out at the vast panorama and even though he had seen this view before, his voice was awed when he spoke. "Nowhere else but in the American wilderness can such a sight be seen!"

But the boys were too weary to enjoy the view or to talk. All they wanted to do was rest and take long drinks of cool, sweet spring water that gurgled down over a mossy, fern-covered rock.

The circuit rider busily prepared for the journey down the mountain. After he examined the harness for breaks and cracks, he fastened a heavy iron chain around the spokes of the two back wheels of the wagon, locking them together.

"With the back wheels dragging, the wagon won't go down the steep road so fast," he explained.

"Won't going down the mountain be easier than climbing up?" John asked hopefully.

Mr. Tom shook his head and answered, "Wait and see!"

They started out, the circuit rider leading the horses slowly down the steep grade. As the boys slipped and slid over loose rocks and stumbled over stumps of trees, John called out, "Now I know what you mean, Mr. Tom!"

The circuit rider looked back and grinned ruefully. "There's nothing easy about going up or down Sideling Hill, Johnny."

Halfway down the mountain a sudden hot wind sprang up and they heard the rumble of thunder.

"Just as I thought," Mr. Tom called from ahead of the wagon. "A storm's brewing, and these mountain storms are nothing to fool around in. We'll try to find a safe place to stop." He grasped Joshua's lead strap tighter and the weary horses continued to move more carefully down the rough slope.

Just as a flash of lightning split through the gray clouds overhead, James spied a ledge of rock back through the trees. He called out to Mr. Tom and pointed to the cavelike shelter. The circuit rider quickly pulled the horses to a stop and the boys ran ahead to help him tie the grays securely to nearby trees. They rolled heavy rocks under each wheel of the wagon to keep it from rolling. By the time all this was done, the rain was coming down in torrents.

Wet through and shivering, they ran for the ledge of rock. Huddled together under the stone shelter, they waited out the storm.

Lightning flashed all around them. Somewhere close by they heard the crash of a tree splitting apart. John crept closer to Mr. Tom. "When's it going to be over?" he asked, trying to keep his voice steady.

"Hush, listen!" James cocked his head suddenly. "What's that?"

Through the noise of the rain drumming on the ledge above, they heard a faint barking sound.

Mr. Tom leaned forward, listening. "It could be a fox barking. It sounds as if it's coming from the road."

When the sound came closer, John cried, "It's a dog!"

The barking grew louder. "It *is* a dog!" exclaimed James. "Maybe it needs help." And before Mr. Tom could stop him, he dashed from the ledge and beat his way through the wet forest back to the road. When he returned, he had a trembling, frightened little dog in his arms.

"Well, now," said Mr. Tom as he bent over the wet, shivering creature, "where did you come from?"

James took off his jacket and rubbed the dog's brown fur dry. After shaking himself several times, the little dog wagged his tail gratefully and sniffed curiously at their feet.

"Can we keep him?" John asked eagerly. "Maybe he'd be a good watchdog."

Mr. Tom smiled and patted the dog. "Well, we can't leave him alone on the mountain. I guess he can travel with us."

"Where do you think he came from?" James wondered.

"Most likely he strayed away from a family traveling over Sideling Hill," the circuit rider replied.

"Well, he's got a new home now," John said, scooping the little dog into his arms and burying his face in its brown furry side.

When the worst of the storm was over, they made their way through the dripping trees back to the road. They removed the stones from under the wagon wheels and untied the horses. With the little dog trotting close to their heels, they were on their way again.

After the heavy rain, the road was worse than ever, but Mr. Tom led them down the rocky way, humming another hymn. The boys sloshed after him through puddles and tried hard not to slip and slide in the muddy ruts. Mr. Tom kept a firm grip on the line as he led the grays around a bend in the road.

Suddenly he drew the horses to a stop and cried out in surprise. There ahead of them was a Conestoga wagon that was having trouble. Lurching sideways down the slippery road, its locked back wheels slid closer and closer to the steep edge. The lead horse, rearing and plunging, was dragging the other horses toward the tree-filled gully below. The driver didn't seem to be anywhere around.

Instinctively, John leaped ahead. All the aching weariness left his legs as he ran past the wagon in trouble and reached up to grasp the bridle of the rearing lead horse. "Whoa, there! Whoa!" he called.

The horse was wild with fear. Its eyes rolled madly and foam fell from its lips. It reared again and came plunging back to earth, nearer and nearer to the edge of the gully.

John threw all his weight against the animal. His feet almost slipped out from under him in the mud but he hung manfully onto the bridle.

Mr. Tom left the care of the two grays to James and hurried ahead to help. The distraught driver picked himself up from the muddy road where he had slipped and fallen and added his weight to the horse. At last the frightened, rearing creature quieted down and the rest of the team was brought into line.

The driver's face was pale. His hand trembled on the bridle as he turned grateful eyes to John and Mr. Tom.

In a panting voice, he said, "My name's David Patterson. I thank you, strangers." Then nodding toward John, he added, "If you hadn't grabbed the bridle when you did, lad, my team and wagon would be down in that gully now. That took a heap of courage."

John blushed and glanced down at his mud-spattered shoes. The man's praise made him happy, but it made him a little uncomfortable too.

Mr. Tom put a hand on his shoulder. "John's a brave lad and has a way with horses," he said. "We're glad to have helped you, Mr. Patterson. But right now we'd better keep going or we'll not get down off this mountain before nightfall. They'll be plenty of time to talk when we camp below."

Mr. Patterson nodded agreement and turned his attention to his team. "I'm just glad I sent my wife and daughter walking on ahead," he said.

All this time the little brown dog had been dancing around the stranger. Now he gave a few sharp barks as if to call attention to himself.

Mr. Patterson looked down suddenly and a smile broke across his troubled face. "Why, Rowdy, where have you been?"

"Is he your dog, sir?" asked John.

The man nodded and reached down to pat the little dog. "We lost him on top of the mountain. Janey, my little girl, will sure be glad to see him."

Mr. Tom told John to stay and help Mr. Patterson with his horses, then he walked back to his own wagon. Mr. Patterson mounted the big wheel horse where he rode to guide his team and John walked alongside the lead horse. He glanced back at the Conestoga. "Your wagon sure is big, sir," he called out admiringly.

"It had to be big to haul all our furniture and household goods," its owner replied. "We aim to settle west over the mountains."

It was almost dark when the road finally leveled out and they reached the bottom of the mountain at last. A steady rain had begun to fall. Mr. Patterson found his wife and small daughter huddled together under a big elm tree to keep dry.

At the sight of her mud-spattered husband, Mrs. Patterson ran from the tree to meet him. Her blond-haired daughter followed, and when she spied Rowdy, she ran to him and kissed his wet furry head.

"Where did you find him, Papa?" she asked.

Pointing to James, her father answered, "This young fellow found him on the road during the storm." And pointing to John, he said, "And this young fellow saved our team from going into a gully up there on the mountain."

The little girl smiled up at the two boys as if they were heroes.

"We are mighty beholden to you," her mother said. "If we could get out of this rain and light a fire, I could repay you by cooking up a meal."

Mr. Tom's blue eyes twinkled. "I think we can accept that invitation, ma'am. There's a settler's cabin not far from here that I have stopped at before."

"Then let's get right to it," Mr. Patterson said without hesitation. He helped his wife and daughter over the big wagon wheel. Then the two wagons started out together, with Rowdy running alongside, barking at the turning wheels.

They had gone scarcely a mile when a pale light greeted them from a cabin alongside the road. Mr.

Tom turned his grays into the small clearing and stopped at the door of the cabin. A woman with a shawl over her head opened the door and peered out through the raindrops.

"Why, it's Mr. Tom," she said. "Come in. Come in."

Mrs. Patterson and Janey scuttled through the rain into the cabin and the two men and boys unhitched the horses and led them into a half-faced log barn behind the house. After the horses were rubbed down, fed, and watered, and Rowdy was tied securely to one of the barn posts, they joined the women.

James and John had never been inside a settler's cabin. They looked curiously around the one large room with its two windows which were covered with greased paper to let in light during the day. A churn, a spinning wheel, and a table of split logs stood on the puncheon floor. Fitted into the walls at one end of the cabin was the bedstead. At the other end of the room was a large stone fireplace above which hung a pair of buck's antlers to hold a long rifle, a bullet pouch, and a powder horn. A blazing fire lighted the entire room.

The boys went straight to the fire to dry their damp clothes. "It's good to have a roof over our heads tonight," Mrs. Patterson said gratefully above the sound of the rain drumming on the clapboards above them.

The woman, whom Mr. Tom introduced as Mrs. Wright, wouldn't take a penny for their lodging. "You can use your own victuals and cook your own supper," she told Mrs. Patterson. "You and the girl can sleep with me in the bed. The men and boys can bed down in the loft. My man's a trapper. He's gone to Bedford to do some trading. It's good to have some company on a stormy night like this."

Mr. Patterson brought in a smoked ham, some cheese, a flitch of bacon, and some cornmeal from his wagon, and Mrs. Patterson began preparing the evening meal. As she bent over the hearth, she reminded James of Mother and how her pretty auburn hair had glowed in the firelight in their little house in Ireland.

The women laid the food out on the split-log table and with noggins of fresh milk and some of Mrs. Wright's homemade molasses cookies, they enjoyed a real feast.

Afterward they sat around the cheery fire and talked. Mr. Tom told about his work as a circuit rider in the back country and explained that James and John were traveling to Pittsburgh with him to join their mother. Then Mr. Patterson told his story. He was a farmer from Reading who was taking his family to a settlement north of Pittsburgh. He had bought some land there and hoped to build a cabin before the first snowfall.

"In the East prices are high and taxes are high," he said. "There just wasn't enough money and I owed so many people. In the Ohio Valley there is good land and cheap. When I get my new farm started, I can pay off my debts and at the same time help settle a new part of the country."

He glanced down at his daughter who had snuggled close to him by the fire. "I only wish there was a school in the settlements for Janey to go to."

"At the rate settlers are moving across the mountains," said Mr. Tom, "it shouldn't be long before schools and churches are built in the western country."

Mrs. Wright nodded. "When we first built our cabin here, we thought it was the loneliest place on earth.

Now it seems that half the world is traveling by our door." Then she asked them about news from the East. Was the waiting long at the ferry across the Susquehanna? What was happening in Philadelphia these days? Was it true that they were going to move the capital of the country from Philadelphia to a place along the Potomac River and call it Federal City?

When all her questions were answered, Mr. Patterson smiled down at his sleeping daughter and said, "It's time for bed. We have another long day ahead of us tomorrow." He paused and glanced over at Mr. Tom. "Since we're both heading west to Pittsburgh, we might as well travel together."

Mr. Tom nodded. "I'd say that would be a fine idea."

Mrs. Wright stood and lifted a large family Bible from the mantel above the hearth. "Before we bed down for the night, I'd be obliged to hear you read the Scriptures, Mr. Tom," she said. "It's been a long time since a preacher's been traveling through."

Mr. Tom opened the Bible across his knees and by the light of the fire he began to read. "God is our refuge and strength, a very present help in trouble—"

Even though he had a powerful voice, Mr. Tom read the Scriptures in a soft, melodious way. He made God seem kind and loving and helpful.

"God is our refuge and strength, a very present help in trouble—" The words lingered in James's mind. Surely God had been their refuge and strength today on Sideling Hill, he thought. And surely God would continue to keep watch over them tomorrow. The road ahead might be full of dangers, but James knew they were in God's hands.

SHAWNEE CABINS

JAMES woke to the smell of bacon frying and coffee brewing the next morning. He turned over on his straw pallet and blinked up at the shadowy bundles of herbs that were hung to dry from the loft rafters. It was snug and warm under the cabin roof. He was about to go back to sleep when he noticed that Mr. Tom and Mr. Patterson were up and gone.

He leaned over and, pulling a piece of straw from his pallet, tickled his brother on the nose until John was awake. John wriggled his nose, pushed away the straw, and made a playful lunge for his brother. The two grappled on the straw ticks until John rolled over and complained, panting, "I give up! I give up! I'm stiff and sore all over. I sure hope we don't have to climb any more mountains like Sideling Hill today."

"Aye, I hope not, either," James replied. "Come on, let's go down. That bacon sure smells good."

The boys climbed down the loft ladder and were greeted by Janey, who was as bright as the new morning. "I beat you up, you sleepyheads," she teased with a saucy toss of her head.

She followed them to the water barrel outside the cabin door. In the light of day, James noticed how the freckles stood out on her pink cheeks and how her honey-colored hair seemed to catch and hold the gleam of sunlight shining on it. She could not be more than seven or eight, he thought, but she seemed right at home with them, chattering away like a curious squirrel as they dashed water over their faces and slicked back their hair.

"Where's Rowdy?" teased John, reaching out to pull one of her yellow braids. "Is he as *rowdy* as ever this morning?"

"He's out in the barn with Papa and Mr. Tom," she answered, ducking under John's hand. "And he's not rowdy this morning. Come on—I'll show you."

But just then Mrs. Patterson came to the door and called the men and children to breakfast. Janey followed the boys into the cabin and squeezed herself between them on the bench by the table. Even though they were sleepyheads and John had teased her, they were still her heroes for finding Rowdy in the storm yesterday.

The women served buckwheat cakes with the bacon and there were noggins of coffee and milk.

"Eat hearty of the syrup," Mrs. Wright told them.

"My man and I boiled our own sap this spring and there's aplenty."

"It sure makes these pancakes taste good," remarked James, who had never tasted maple syrup before. Both he and John ate six cakes apiece.

As soon as breakfast was over and the horses were hitched to the wagons, the travelers prepared to leave. But before they said good-bye to their hostess, Mrs. Patterson brought out a fine linen handkerchief from her trunk and handed it to Mrs. Wright.

A nostalgic look came into the woman's eyes as she touched the delicate lace on the handkerchief with her rough, work-worn hands. "I've not had such a pretty thing as this since I was a girl in Philadelphia," she said. And turning to the packet of salt Mr. Tom gave her, she added, "Salt is so scarce west of the mountains that we call it white gold. Settlers and Indians would trade most anything for a handful of salt."

She thanked them for their gifts then stood in the middle of the road and waved until the wagons dipped down over a rise and were out of sight.

As they rode along, the boys joined Mr. Tom in his hymn singing. Nobody minded that the road was still muddy and full of ruts. It was a pleasant day. The rain had cooled the humid forest air and a light breeze rippled through the trees along the way. The valley road was fairly level and they all had a chance to ride, even Rowdy, whom Janey kept close to her on the wagon seat so that he wouldn't get lost again.

The wooded valley was full of game. "No wonder Mr. Wright, being a trapper, chose this place to live," the circuit rider told them between hymns. "Just look at that tree full of squirrels up ahead."

The further they went, the more squirrels they saw. There were gray squirrels and black squirrels, hopping all over the ground and leaping through the branches of trees almost in swarms.

Rowdy barked wildly and the boys giggled as they listened in the wagon behind. Janey would have a time keeping a tight hold on her little brown dog today.

By night fall when they stopped to camp, Mr. Patterson had shot enough squirrels for their meal. Mrs. Patterson rolled the meat in cornmeal and fried it to a crisp. James thought he had never tasted anything so good.

"I never saw so many squirrels in my life," Mr. Patterson declared after they had eaten and were sitting around the campfire, talking. "They seem to be migrating east. Now why would they do that?"

"I heard tell there's been a drought over the mountains this summer," Mr. Tom replied, "and there's a scarcity of nuts and acorns."

No sooner had he spoken than he held up his hand as a signal to be quiet. They strained their ears. At first they heard nothing except the horses cropping grass along the bank of the spring and now and then one of them stamping and whinnying. Then came a faint, wailing cry from somewhere in the forest.

Mrs. Patterson put her hands to her throat. "Why, it sounds like a little child lost in the woods!"

"Maybe we better go hunt for it," Mr. Patterson said, getting up to light a brand from the fire. But Mr. Tom stopped him.

"I'd say that cry came from a panther kitten and the mother isn't far away," he warned. "The horses sense it and are uneasy."

92

Mr. Patterson dropped the brand into the fire and turned quickly. "John and I better bring them closer to camp and double their fastenings."

"And James and I will build up the fire," said Mr. Tom.

John followed Mr. Patterson to where the horses were tied and led the two grays close to the fire which James and Mr. Tom now had blazing.

The faint, wailing sounded closer. Suddenly they heard the awe-some, bloodcurdling cry of its mother nearby, and knew for sure that Mr. Tom was right.

James and John were badly frightened. Never before had they heard anything like that screaming cry. The horses whinnied in terror and Janey buried her face in her hands to shut out the sound.

Mr. Tom slipped over beside her. "Now, don't let that mama panther frighten you, Janey," he told her. "If she should come into our camp, we'll put a wee bit of salt on her tail and that will calm her down."

Janey peeked through her fingers, her eyes wide with wonder. "It would?"

The laughter that followed broke the tension of the moment and even Janey was smiling.

They kept throwing more wood on the fire until it blazed high, and soon the cries in the night became fainter as the panther and her kitten moved on.

The moon was high in the sky when they finally bedded down for the night. The Patterson slept in the big covered wagon while Mr. Tom and the boys rolled up in their blankets close to the fire. In almost no time at all they were sound asleep and nothing bothered them again for the rest of that night.

The next morning they forded the Juniata River and

stopped in the town of Bedford to have the horses' shoes looked after before the long climb up the Allegheny Mountain. While they waited their turn at the blacksmith shop, the boys and Janey walked around the town.

Bedford was the largest town between Sideling Hill and Pittsburgh. Wagons and carriages filled the main street and the stores were crowded with settlers buying provisions and farm tools before they continued the journey westward.

A pony express rider jogged by, his saddlebags filled with mail from Pittsburgh. Pack trains traveling east were loaded with animal skins and ginseng to be traded for goods to bring back over the mountains.

When the children finally wandered back to the blacksmith shop, the horses were ready and they were all soon on their way again. The road westward led over gently rising land and through deep natural meadows. Toward the middle of the afternoon the boys became tired of riding and decided to walk on ahead to look for a place to camp for the night. They had walked for about a mile when a strange noise made them stop dead still.

"That sounds like a drum," exclaimed John, "and it's nearby."

"Let's tell Mr. Tom," James said, and the two boys raced back to the wagons.

"That's an Indian drum," Mr. Tom told them when they stopped the horses to listen, "and it's coming from Shawnee cabins."

Mrs. Patterson gave a little cry and clasped her hands together.

"No need to fear, ma'am," Mr. Tom assured her.

"The Shawnees are peaceful now. They are traders and some of them speak English. They'll let us camp in their village tonight and tomorrow we'll trade salt for buckskins and moccasins."

James and John looked at one another excitedly. They had never seen American Indians before, but they had heard exciting tales about them.

The sounding drum led them to an open glade where they glimpsed a scattering of log houses and bark wigwams. Mr. Tom called a halt, climbed down over the wagon wheel, and started across the glade. Several Indian men stepped forward dressed in leather breechclouts with turkey and eagle feathers in their long, black hair.

Mr. Tom held out the palms of his hands in a greeting of friendship and the Indians did the same. He pointed back to the wagons and the Indians showed them a sheltered place where the travelers could camp.

"Tonight we feast," one of the Shawnees said. "Hunters come home with much venison and turkey. Chief says strangers welcome to feast. Hunting gods pleased when strangers eat."

Mrs. Patterson hesitated and looked fearfully at her husband, but Mr. Patterson smiled down at her. Taking her hand and Janey's, he led them to the Indian fire in the middle of the glade.

When everyone had gathered in a circle around the fire, the drums stopped beating. The Shawnee women passed around wooden platters of venison and turkey, followed by bowls of succotash and potatoes. The boys found the Indian food delicious and stuffed themselves, much to the delight of their Shawnee hosts.

Janey had made friends with one of the Indian girls. Although they couldn't understand each other's words, they sat giggling together all through the meal.

When the feast was over, the chief arose and addressed the gathering in the Shawnee language. He was a tall, brown, handsome man dressed in a deerskin hunting shirt richly embroidered with beadwork. He held his head proudly and spoke with dignity. Now and then he would turn and gesture to the white guests.

"He is welcoming us to their feast," Mr. Tom leaned over and whispered to the boys. "When treated respectfully, redmen are the most generous people on earth."

When the chief finished speaking, everyone played games together to celebrate the feast. The boys shot arrows at a bear's paw that was fastened to a pole.

John joined the archers. He had to be shown how to bend the bow and notch the arrow to the bowstring. When he drew back on the bow, his arrow went wobbling through the air far from its mark. The Indian boys laughed, but John goodnaturedly tried again and again until he finally managed to hit the pole.

The older boys had wrestling contests. A boy James's age motioned for him to wrestle. James eyed the boy anxiously. He was shorter than James but his shoulders were broader. The chief gave an order and the boys moved closer together. It wasn't long before James was pinned to the ground. His young opponent, Little Cat, reached out a hand to help him up.

The games ended with a race. The course was from one end of the meadow to the other and back again. Two judges were posted at each end of the meadow.

James saw Little Cat walking jauntily toward the line of runners and followed him. Fifteen boys had entered the race. At the signal, the line of running boys surged forward across the field.

John and Mr. Tom and the Pattersons stood with the spectators and cheered James on. He was easy to spot, for his light brown hair stood out among all the other dark-haired runners.

Soon the wide line narrowed as the better runners moved ahead. James was moving up. John knew his brother had always been a good runner and had won many school races in Ireland. He and Janey jumped up and down, cheering him on. James ran harder than ever. After the beating he had taken at the wrestling match, he wanted to show Little Cat that a white boy could run, too.

Little Cat was ahead of him when they reached the end of the meadow. But James didn't lose heart. He knew that the Indian boy was running too fast and not pacing himself. On the way back across the meadow James kept up the same steady pace. He was passing most of the front runners now. Little Cat glanced around and saw James gaining on him. He tried to run faster, but his breath was getting short and his legs were beginning to feel like blocks of wood.

Now the two boys were ahead, running neck to neck, James still keeping his steady, even pace. Just before the finish line, he gave a final burst of speed that he had reserved for the end and pulled ahead of Little Cat. He reached the finish line first and collapsed on the grass behind it. Little Cat, panting and limping, sank down on the grass beside him.

The Shawnees cheered the white boy as if he had

been one of their own, and Little Cat and James looked at each other and laughed.

"Good race," Little Cat said in English.

"Good fight," James replied.

With arms around each other's necks, the Indian boy and the white boy walked off together to watch the dancing around the campfire.

The Shawnees danced in a circle, counterclockwise, the men leading off and the women closing in behind. The women danced gracefully, moving one foot lightly forward and then backward to the rhythm of the drum. They held their bodies straight, their arms hanging relaxed and close to their bodies. Toward the end of the dance some of the younger men stomped their feet vigorously, making fantastic leaps and turns, their movements punctuated with shrill cries.

During one dance a hunter with a bow and arrow danced alone around the fire, acting out his experiences on the hunt that day. He shuffled about in a circle as if he were stalking game. Then he flapped his arms and gobbled like a wild turkey. Notching his arrow to the bowstring, he sent it flying up through the night air. His dance ended in a shrill cry of triumph as he bagged his game.

The dancing continued well into the night. Long after the travelers had returned to their wagons, they could hear the echoes of the drumbeat and the monotonous chanting of the dancers.

Before they said good-bye to their Shawnee hosts the next morning, Mr. Tom traded packets of salt for moccasins and hunting shirts. The boys couldn't wait to shed their old clothes for new buckskin shirts and fringed breeches.

Each boy's hunting shirt was loose and reached halfway down his thighs. Folded part way around itself when belted, it left ample space in the bosom for a chest pocket for carrying things. James put the six silver spoons in his bosom pocket where they would carry well, and John put the money Mrs. Jenkins had given them and the folding knife in his.

"Look, our shirts are even embroidered with beadwork, like the chief's." John exclaimed with delight.

"And our pants are fringed like Mr. Tom's," James added.

But most of all, they couldn't wait to kick off their worn shoes and put on the soft Indian moccasins. Mr. Tom told them to fill the moccasins with moss and grass.

"It makes walking that much easier," he said, glancing ahead at the towering ranges to the west, "and we'll need as soft footwear as we can get when we climb Allegheny Mountain tomorrow."

FIRE!

"I wouldn't mind being an Indian," John said as they headed toward Allegheny Mountain the next day. "They seem to have all the fun!" The travelers had been talking about their good time at Shawnee Cabins. Even Mrs. Patterson had enjoyed the visit.

"Living does seem easier for redmen than for white settlers," Mr. Tom agreed. "Maybe it's because they live at harmony with nature and are not trying to change it or work against it all the time."

"Aye," John said wistfully, "they don't bother to chop down trees or milk cows or work hard for a living. They just pick out a nice green meadow and settle down and hunt for their food."

Mr. Tom laughed. "Well, hunting can be hard work, too, Johnny, but they go about it with happy hearts and they never kill more game than they can eat. To them the deer and the turkey are their brothers and have as much right to live as they."

The group rode along in silence for awhile. Then James asked, "How far do we have to go until we reach Pittsburgh, Mr. Tom?"

The circuit rider shook the reins for the horses to go faster. "We have Allegheny Mountain to cross and then Laurel Ridge and Chestnut Ridge," he replied. "After Chestnut Ridge the going is easy and we're almost there."

When the road began climbing the foothills of Allegheny Mountain, the boys jumped off the wagon seat and walked beside the horses. Behind them Mr. Tom called, "Gee, Joshua—gee, Job—gee there!"

As they climbed the steep, winding road that twisted upward toward the summit, John exclaimed happily, "These Indian moccasins sure make walking easier. My feet don't ache half as much as they did before."

At the summit they stopped to rest the horses and wait for the big Conestoga behind them.

"The English established a fort here on top of the mountain during the French and Indian War," Mr. Tom told the boys. "That was back in 1758 when General Forbes built this road to the forks of the Ohio."

James looked around but all he saw were trees and bushes. "I don't see any fort."

"The timbers have probably fallen down and a thicket has grown up around the foundations," Mr.

Tom said. He pointed in the direction of a little spring they heard gurgling out of the rocks. "It was built near that spring."

Forgetting their weary climb up the mountain, the boys leaped through the bushes in the direction of the spring to search for the fort. When the Patterson wagon rumbled to a stop at the summit, Rowdy scrambled down from Janey's lap and gamboled after them. The sound of gurgling water had led the boys to the old log walls of the palisade. They walked through the gate and into the yard of the fort which was now guarded by a thicket of underbrush. Several crude log huts still remained but they, too, were buried by the forest growth, their moss-covered roofs rotted and caved in.

Rowdy sniffed his way through the thicket, then raised his voice in a series of urgent barks. John ran to see what the little dog had found.

"Hey, look at this!" he exclaimed as he reached down and picked up a long shaft of wood, feathered at one end and pointed with a flint arrowhead at the other. "An Indian arrow! Do you suppose the fort was attacked by Indians?"

James leaped over a laurel bush to inspect his brother's find. "Aye, maybe it was. Let's ask Mr. Tom."

When the circuit rider examined the arrow, he said, "It could be a war arrow or maybe an Indian hunter was chasing a deer through the old fort and his arrow missed its mark."

"May we keep it?" John asked eagerly.

Mr. Tom nodded. "I don't see why not."

Janey, who had come to see what the boys had

found, shook her head with disgust. "Why do you want to keep an old Indian arrow?"

"We never saw one before," John told her. "In Ireland where we come from there are no forts nor Indians."

"But we do have round stone towers on top of our hills and old castles to guard our coast," James added.

"Do pretty princesses live in the castles and are they guarded by dragons?" asked the girl, her eyes big and round.

James laughed and tweaked her yellow braids. "Not anymore. That's just found in fairy tales and old legends."

"Well, enough of fairy tales and legends," said Mr. Patterson. "We'd better get started down the mountain."

After they had carried buckets of water from the spring for the horses and filled their own canteens, they were ready to start out again. At the western foot of the ridge they crossed a high, dry plateau between the mountains that Mr. Tom said was known as the Glades. The trees and bushes along the road were withered a dusty green and the air hung still and heavy. The sun was hot and burned down unmercifully on the travelers.

Now and then Mr. Tom pointed to leaves on trees that were shriveled and brown and remarked how dry the forest was.

James remembered the hundreds of squirrels they had seen migrating eastward because of the drought in the mountains. As he glanced around at the dry forest, he understood now why there would be a scarcity of nuts and acorns on the western slopes this fall.

103

They camped that night by Stony Creek at the foot of a wooded bluff. Mr. Tom told them that it was one of the largest streams in the Glades, but now there were only a succession of deep pools and thin streams of water trickling over the stones.

After supper they gathered around the fire for Mr. Tom's Bible reading. They were listening intently to David's fight with the giant Goliath when suddenly the circuit rider stopped reading and looked up sharply. He glanced across the creek for a moment, listening. Then he closed his Bible and hurried to the top of the bluff on the other side. Mr. Patterson followed close behind him.

As the others sat by the campfire, listening, they became aware of a dull roar from the dark forest beyond. Rowdy, sensing something was wrong, shivered and growled nervously.

The men came splashing back across the creek, shouting as they came. The forest to the west was on fire, they said, and the wall of flame was traveling rapidly toward them. There was not a moment to lose.

At Mr. Tom's command, the boys raced to where the horses were hobbled and led them into the deeper pools in the creek. They tied the frightened animals securely to tree trunks overhanging the bank, and Mrs. Patterson brought some empty grain sacks which she tied over the horses' eyes so that they couldn't see. Then they all helped Mr. Tom and Mr. Patterson push the wagons down the bank into the creek.

The terrible fire raced down the wooded bluff toward the creek. The boys tied wet handkerchiefs around their faces as the wall of flame swept toward them.

They dashed buckets of water over the canvas tops until each wagon top was saturated. As they worked, a hot wind sprang up with the approaching flames. Suddenly Janey dropped her bucket and screamed, "Look!"

She was pointing to a strange procession of creatures which had emerged from the woods on the opposite side of the creek. First some rabbits and other small animals, frightened by the roar of the fire behind them, scampered across the stream. Then came foxes and raccoons and next a very strange sight. A large panther came loping along with a herd of deer.

A big black bear lumbered by and at its heels, side by side, a lynx and a pretty fawn were racing to avoid the fury behind them. Intent about their own safety, the animals forgot their fear of one another and were rushing together toward the safety of the forests beyond.

James looked up and saw the air filled with hundreds of birds. Frightened from their perches in the trees, they fluttered about aimlessly, uttering strange, wild cries.

Above the noise and confusion of the birds, Mr. Patterson shouted, "Mother, you and Janey and Rowdy get into the wagon and stay there. Wrap these wet handkerchiefs around your noses and mouths."

Janey was white-faced and scared. She clung to her mother with one hand and to Rowdy with the other.

"Oh, dear God, protect us," cried Mrs. Patterson. "What about the rest of you?"

"We'll be close by and we'll be all right, Mother," Mr. Patterson assured her.

Mr. Tom turned to the boys. "Splash water over

106

yourselves," he commanded, "and be sure your hair is soaking wet. Then lie, face down along the bank and remain there until the fire passes."

The boys splashed themselves with buckets of water. Ordinarily it would have been fun after such a hot day, but they weren't laughing and shouting as they usually did at such a frolic. They hurried to get wet through; then, as the circuit rider had commanded, they lay face down along the bank of the creek between the two men.

James's heart pounded as he listened to the roar of the fire drawing closer. He lifted his head slightly and saw John crouched next to him, his hands clasped tightly as if he were praying. James felt a prayer rise in his own throat. "Dear God, watch over us," he murmured.

He felt Mr. Tom's comforting hand on his shoulder. "Keep your head down, James, and don't worry. The Lord *will* watch over us."

Now began the first terrible sounds of the coming terror, a roar that sounded like thunder as the fire raced down their side of the wooded bluff toward the creek. The loud snapping of dry tree branches sounded like the cracking of rawhide whips. The fiery explosion of a hollow tree echoed like the booming of a cannon.

The boys tied their wet handkerchiefs around their noses and mouths and closed their eyes tightly as the wall of flame swept down upon them. Vaguely they were aware of the terrified snorts and the plunging sounds of the poor horses in the midst of the blaze. James prayed that their ropes would hold.

The fire was checked by the creek, but there was one intense moment when James felt almost stifled with the hot, smoky air and it seemed as if his flesh were shriveling up.

A wild flaming light flared up as the fierce rush of flames passed over them. Then the hot air rose and James's tense body relaxed as the cold night air rushed in to fill the vacuum.

He raised his head slightly to look around. The others lay as still as wet logs along the creek bank. When they were sure the last of the flames had passed over them, one by one they arose slowly, helping each other to his feet.

They looked around them. The worst of the fire had passed but the danger was not over. The bushes and the grass along the road were still burning and Mr. Tom's wagon was smoking ominously.

While the circuit rider ran to his wagon and Mr. Patterson splashed into the creek to see about Janey and Mrs. Patterson, the boys flung buckets of water onto the burning bushes and grass. When the flames died out, they went to check the horses.

The animals were somewhat singed but not burned badly. Still blinded with the grain sacks, they stood trembling in the middle of the pools. The boys calmed the frightened creatures as best they could then untied the blinds and threw water on their hot smoky backs.

Rowdy greeted everybody with anxious, whining barks as Janey and Mrs. Patterson emerged shakily from the big wagon. They had nearly suffocated from the heat of the flames, but otherwise they were fine. Mr. Tom stamped out the burning ember that had fallen into his wagon and announced that not much damage had been done.

"We were lucky indeed," Mr. Patterson said gravely

as he wiped his hot, sooty face with the back of his hand.

"Not just lucky," James declared. "Mr. Tom said the Lord would watch over us and He did."

Janey broke the solemnity of the moment by clapping her hands over her mouth to smother her giggles.

"I don't see anything so funny," John said puzzled, slightly annoyed by the girl's sudden mirth.

Janey laughed outright. "You would if you could see yourselves."

In the light from her father's lantern they noticed, for the first time, that they were covered from head to foot with mud and soot. Only the whites of their eyes showed.

"I guess we men had better clean up some," said Mr. Tom, grinning.

Mrs. Patterson sent Janey to the wagon for some soap. Then with buckets of water from the creek, they scrubbed themselves clean.

After the excitement of the forest fire, it was a long time before they could settle down to sleep. Even Janey was wide-eyed and wide-awake. She wanted to tell of her and Rowdy's experiences in the wagon during the fire, and then for a time they all talked about their own impressions of the blaze. But finally the little camp grew quiet. Even though the air was still filled with the smell of charred wood and the sky to the west still glowed a bright pink where the fire had started, they all fell into an exhausted sleep.

THE LAST RIDGE

THE FOREST they traveled through the next morning was desolate looking. The fire had scorched the earth in a wide black swath over the wooded bluff across Stony Creek. Along the road charred tree trunks still smoldered like tall sooty chimneys, and a pall of smoke hung over everything. The fire had swept over the entire forest to the west and was only now burning itself out in a rocky region among the foothills of Laurel Ridge where trees and underbrush were scarce.

As they started up the ridge road, the sky clouded over and a light rain began to fall.

"I'll warrant this is the first rain in this part of the country for many weeks," Mr. Patterson said. "After yesterday, I'll not complain about traveling in rain."

When they reached the summit, it was shrouded in mist so thick that the trees and bushes around them made dim ghostly shadows. They lingered only long enough to eat a hasty lunch of cold ham and corn pone before they started down the western side of the ridge.

James noticed that his brother had hardly touched his food, and on the way down the ridge, John had hardly spoken two words. "What's the matter, Johnny?" he asked.

"I have a toothache," his brother replied. "It's just a dull pain. Maybe it'll go away."

But by the time they reached the valley below, his tooth was throbbing and his cheek was beginning to swell. Poor John could hardly keep back the tears.

Mrs. Patterson sorted through her herb bag and found some calamus root for him to chew. She told him to lie back in the wagon, but the calamus root didn't help much and the jolting of the wagon made the toothache worse.

"There's a blacksmith in the Ligonier Valley who can pull teeth faster than any barber in Philadelphia," Mr. Tom said, trying to console the boy. "His name is John McDowell and his blacksmith shop is right along the road. We should reach it by nightfall."

They rode on, passing gently sloping woodlands and meadows where cabins and farmland had been carved out of the forest. At Laughlintown they passed the first roadside inn they had seen since Bedford.

It was getting dark when they reached John McDowell's blacksmith shop. The smith was just closing up for the night as they drew up in front of it. He came out to see what they wanted.

"If it was just a horse wantin' a shoe, I'd say you could wait till mornin'," the weary smith said. "But a toothache can't wait. Come in, laddie. It won't take long."

John never had a tooth pulled before. He followed the blacksmith into his dark, cavernous shop reluctantly. Mr. McDowell lighted a lantern and told James to hold it up so that he could see. The smith sorted through the tools on his bench and found an iron instrument that looked like a large door key with a hook at the end. "Now open your mouth, lad, and point to the tooth that aches."

John opened wide and pointed to a back tooth.

"Sit down here on the anvil and Mr. Tom can hold your head. I'll have that tooth out quicker'n you can say your name."

John was trembling all over when the blacksmith clamped the iron hook around the aching tooth. He looked up fearfully at Mr. Tom, but the circuit rider gave him an encouraging wink and held his head steady. After several painful tugs and a powerful yank the tooth was out.

"Ow!" John yelled, holding the side of his face. "Ow, it hurts worse than ever."

Mr. McDowell laughed. "How can it when it's out? Look, here it is and it's yours to keep."

John stopped yelling and looked at the bloody tooth. "I don't want it," he said. "You can throw it away."

"I don't blame you for not wantin' it," the smith said. "You're better off without it."

Mr. Tom offered to pay Mr. McDowell, but the friendly smith just shook his head. "Tomorrow's the Sabbath and if you'd be willin' to have a meeting for us, that will be payment enough. You know my wife'll be glad to put you up for the night, and I'll round up the neighbors. They'll all be mighty proud to hear some real preachin' again."

It was good to sleep under a roof that night. By morning John's jaw had stopped throbbing and he was feeling fine. After the neighboring settlers crowded into the blacksmith's large cabin, Mr. Tom conducted the Sabbath meeting. When the preaching and singing were over, the men set up benches and a long table of planks outside in the dooryard. The women loaded the table with the food they had brought for the meeting—hams and beef and potatoes and greens, with pies for dessert. As Mrs. Patterson joined the other women in preparing the meal, she looked happier than the boys had ever seen her on the journey. And when they said good-bye to everybody and started up the road again, she had a contented smile of her face.

"If all the folks in the western country are as friendly as these folks in the Ligonier Valley, I'll be happy in my new home," she declared.

At the end of the next day's journey when they reached the summit of Chestnut Ridge, they caught their first glimpse of the western country. The boys who had hiked up the mountain ahead of the others, reached the summit first. At the crest they found a natural clearing which gave them a good view of the countryside.

"Oh, Johnny, look!" gasped James as they stood on the last ridge of the great Appalachian Mountains and viewed the panorama before them. The tall mountains were behind them now and westward, as far as they could see, spread a vast expanse of rolling country covered with virgin woodland. Except for the shrill cry of a lone eagle soaring against the sky, all was silent and undisturbed. Away stretched endless blue hills blending into a peach-colored sunset along the distant horizon. The boys stared in awe at the vast western landscape, feeling the thrilling power of the scene before them.

When the wagons arrived and the others viewed the panorama, they too were impressed and Mrs. Patterson murmured, "We are like Moses on the mount, getting a view of the Promised Land."

A bright full moon floated in the evening sky that night, covering the misty mountaintop in a silvery blanket.

"Before another full moon we'll be at our new home," the boys heard Mr. Patterson tell his family as they settled down for the night.

The next day they descended their last mountain, and now the road dipped steadily downward over low rolling hills to the Ohio Valley. Everybody was in a festive mood as they rode along. Mr. Tom sang one hymn after another. Rowdy, who was trotting alongside the Patterson wagon, began to weave in and out between the horses' feet. Once in awhile he would nip the fetlocks to hurry them along. John, who was driving Joshua and Job, flicked the snake whip over the grays' heads and they trotted along briskly as if they knew that they would soon reach their destination and the long journey would be over.

As they neared Pittsburgh, the traveling was less lonely than it had been on the mountain roads. The call of voices and the sounds of horses were all around them now. At night when they camped, it was comforting to see the light of other campfires nearby. Sometimes they could hear fiddles playing and voices singing. Once as James and John listened to a fiddler play a tender, lilting song from Ireland, they felt as homesick for their native country as the fiddler must have felt who played it.

One afternoon when they stopped on a rise of land to rest the horses, Mr. Tom pointed to a long river valley that stretched out before them. "Look ahead," he called out, pointing with his snake whip. "That's the Ohio Valley."

They all turned to stare at the deep river valley below them. It was a beautiful sight. Between high wooded ridges, on a point of land shaped like an arrowhead, two rivers joined to form one large river flowing westward.

Mr. Tom pointed to the river to their left. "That muddy-looking river is called the Monongahela and the winding river you see to the right is the Allegheny. They join at the Point to form the Ohio."

"What funny names those are for rivers," exclaimed Janey.

"The Delaware Indians named them," Mr. Tom replied. "Monongahela means 'muddy water,' Allegheny means 'great warpath,' and the Ohio means 'beautiful water.' The Indians pronounce Ohio 'Ho-hee-yo.' "

Janey and the boys laughed and said "Ho-hee-yo" over and over again.

"Now we can talk Indian," John said. "When I see another Indian, I'm going to say 'Ho-hee-yo' and he'll know what I mean."

Mr. Tom then pointed to the point of land where a cluster of houses stood. "Now see those houses at the point where the three rivers meet?" he said. "Well, that's Pittsburgh."

The boys stared intently at the little town nestled in the forks of the Ohio. Their hearts beat rapidly and their eyes glowed with excitement. They had reached their destination at last. Somewhere down there where the three rivers meet, they'd find Mother.

PITTSBURGH

IT WAS late afternoon when they rode through the dusty streets of Pittsburgh. The children glanced around them eagerly. In 1800 Pittsburgh still had the look of a frontier town. Unlike Philadelphia, most of its houses were made of logs and only now and then did they pass a more comfortable home built of brick or stone.

The First Presbyterian Church on Wood and Sixth streets and the small brick German Reformed Church on the corner of Sixth and Smithfields streets had no elegant towers or steeples like the churches in Philadelphia. Chickens pecked at bits of grain that had fallen from wagons alongside the road. As they turned down Market Street, the boys had to climb down from the wagon to shoo off a cow that stood in the middle of the road.

On the corner of Ferry Street along the Monongahela River, Mr. Tom drew the horses to a stop in front of a big two-story tavern with a sign, "Samuel Semples Tavern," hanging in front.

"This is a good place to stay," he called back to the Pattersons, who planned to spend the night in Pittsburgh before going on to their claim the next day.

Mr. Patterson climbed off the wheel horse and walked over to the circuit rider's wagon. "We owe you and the boys so much for helping us out on Sideling Hill, Mr. Tom, that I'd like to treat you all to dinner in the tavern."

Before the circuit rider could reply, Janey cried out, "Oh, please, Mr. Tom."

"It will be our last night together," her mother urged. "We can't just say good-bye here like this."

Mr. Tom turned to James and John. "The tavern is a good place to ask about your mother," he suggested. "Samuel Semples meets many new settlers who come to Pittsburgh."

"Then we'll come!" they agreed eagerly.

"Oh, goodie!" Janey exclaimed, dancing up and down on the wagon seat.

"Careful, daughter," her father said as he reached up for her, "you'd better do your jig down here before you fall and break your pretty little neck."

Mr. Tom helped Mrs. Patterson over the big front wheel while James and John held the horses. After the wagons were driven into the stable yard and Rowdy was tied to one of the wagon wheels, the men and boys

118

joined Mrs. Patterson and Janey inside the tavern.

The one large room was crowded with travelers on their way to the settlements, and they had to wait for a place at one of the heavy oak tables. As John watched a serving girl bring the food to the tables, he suddenly felt so hungry that he thought their turn to eat would never come. His mouth watered as he stared at the red bowls piled high with mountains of snowy, whipped potatoes and the platters filled with rosy baked ham and fat roasted chickens. There were loaves of warm bread fresh from the oven, dishes of corn, and bowls of apple sauce. The innkeeper's plump wife was on her knees, taking golden brown berry pies from the oven alongside the fireplace. It had been a long time since John had seen food like this being served.

At last Samuel Semples, the gray-haired genial host, led them to an empty table and they all sat down to eat. The tavern keeper was a busy man that evening. It wasn't until after they had eaten and were gathered around the huge fireplace at the end of the room that Mr. Tom had a chance to ask him about James and John's mother.

Mr. Semples looked thoughtful, then slowly shook his head. "So many new people pass through Pittsburgh these days, that I can't remember," he said. "You say she left Philadelphia over a year ago?"

"Yes, sir," James spoke up. "She came here to find a man named Malcolm McPherson. It's on his land that we are to settle."

Mr. Semple's brows furrowed as he studied the flames in the hearth. "There are many Irishmen with the name McPherson around here, but I don't know of one called Malcolm."

Noticing the boys' downcast look, he added quickly, "Don't worry, lads. Your mother could be right here in Pittsburgh and I wouldn't know it, with all these settlers coming and going. But I know of a man in Pittsburgh who could help you find her better than I."

James looked up eagerly. "Who's that, sir?" he asked.

"George Adams, who lives on the corner of Redoubt Alley and First Street. The post office is in his home. He knows just about everybody in Pittsburgh."

"We'll see him when the post office opens first thing in the morning," Mr. Tom assured the boys. "And until we find your mother, you can stay with me at my sister's house."

It was getting late and time for Mr. Tom and the boys to leave. Janey, with tear-blurred eyes, cried, "I don't want James and John to leave. Can't they come with us?"

"They must find their mother," Mrs. Patterson told her. "She is as lonely for them as I would be for you if I hadn't seen you for a whole year."

James felt his throat tighten as he took a step forward to give the little girl a hug. "Good-bye, Janey," he said, trying to sound cheerful. "Maybe sometime John and I can come visit you."

"Oh, that would be nice!" Janey exclaimed, her blue eyes shining once more. "Promise you'll do that, Jamie. Promise!"

"I promise," James told her.

"Take care of Rowdy," John said. "Don't let him get lost again."

When the last good-byes were said, Mr. Tom and the boys left Semples Tavern. As they rode through the dark streets of Pittsburgh, the three fell silent. It had been hard saying good-bye to friends with whom they had shared so much while traveling over the mountains. "It's almost as hard saying good-bye to new friends as to old ones," James said with a sigh.

Not far from the tavern, Mr. Tom drew the grays to a halt in front of a log house on Third Street. He led the way to the door and knocked on it. In a few seconds the bar lifted and the door opened. A man exclaimed in a surprised voice, "Why, Tom, you're home!" He turned and called over his shoulder, "Ada, Tom's back."

The man led them into a small comfortable parlor where two children were sitting on the settle next to their mother. A girl, about John's age, and her small brother jumped up and ran to the circuit rider.

"Uncle Tom! Uncle Tom!" they cried joyfully.

"Nancy—Freddy!" And Mr. Tom whirled them around in his strong arms.

Mr. Tom's sister, Ada Evans, arose to greet them. She wore a white kerchief over a brown homespun gown and a frilled mobcap over her light hair. She was as short and fair as Mr. Tom was tall and dark. Only their bright blue eyes matched.

As they sat around the fire in the cozy little parlor, Mr. Tom told his sister and her husband, Abner Evans, about his trip east and how he happened to meet James and John.

"You are welcome to stay with us as long as you like," Ada Evans told the boys, reaching over and giving their hands a motherly pat. "You can sleep with Tom and Freddie in the loft tonight."

Mr. Evans was anxious to hear the news from the

East. While the two men talked, Mrs. Evans led the boys and Freddie up to the loft, where she spread two extra straw pallets on the floor. It was warm and stuffy in the loft, and Freddie ran to open the one window.

"You can see Hogg's Pond from here," he told the boys. "That's where we go fishing."

James looked out the window and saw the moonlight shining on a long pond not far from the cabin. A few houses stood on the other side of the pond and a high hill rose up behind them.

After Mrs. Evans heard Freddie's prayers, she told them good-night and took the candle with her to the room below. Soon the house was quiet. James listened to his brother's deep, steady breathing on the straw pallet beside him. As usual John had fallen asleep at once. But James lay awake, blinking up at the shadowy bunches of herbs that hung from the loft rafters. Their long journey was over and they were in Pittsburgh at last. Tomorrow they would look for Mother. He hoped that somewhere nearby she lay sleeping, too.

The next day, as soon as the post office was open, they went to George Adams's house. Nancy and Freddie tagged along. The postmaster was sorting a stack of letters that settlers who had arrived at Pittsburgh were sending back East to their families. He looked up to see what they wanted.

"Hello, Mr. Tom," he said. "Do you want to send a letter or have you come for one?"

"I have no letters to mail today nor have I come for one, George," Mr. Tom told the postmaster. "But I have come to ask you if you know the whereabouts of these boys' mother."

"What would her name be?" asked the postmaster.

"Mary Graham," Mr. Tom replied.

Mr. Adams frowned and thought for a minute, then shook his head slowly. "I don't recollect a woman by that name living here in Pittsburgh," he replied and the boys' hearts fell. "But then, there are so many new folks coming and going these days that she could be here and I wouldn't know it."

"But our mother has been in Pittsburgh for over a year," John said.

"Aye, and she was to write to us," James added. "Are you sure she didn't mail a letter here?"

Again the postmaster shook his head. "I don't recollect. But maybe she gave it to Mike Higgins, the post rider. I'll ask him when he returns from his trip to Philadelphia. He should be in town any day now." Mr. Adams looked back at the stack of letters he was sorting and shook his head. "He'll have a pile of mail to take back East with him when he rides out again."

The boys were gloomy as they left the post office. "Now what'll we do?" James's voice was husky. "Nobody seems to know about our mother."

John looked forlorn and tried to keep back the tears of disappointment which stung his eyelids. He had so hoped that this very morning they would be with Mother again.

"Don't lose hope," Mr. Tom told them. "I'll go over to the courthouse and see if I can find where Malcolm McPherson's claim is located. Maybe your mother is with the McPhersons."

James's eyes brightened. "I hadn't thought of that. Anyway, if anybody would know where Mother is, the McPhersons would."

Mr. Tom gave him a reassuring pat on the shoulder. "It'll take some time at the courthouse, so why don't you let Nancy and Freddy show you around. There are many interesting things to see in Pittsburgh."

Encouraged by Mr. Tom's words, the boys followed Nancy and Freddie down the street in the opposite direction. For the rest of the morning they explored the town. First they walked along the Monongahela River, where they watched the boats on the river.

"So many boats leave here with settlers for the Ohio country that Pa says Pittsburgh is being called the Gateway to the West," Nancy said proudly.

Small skiffs and bark canoes, piled high with trappers' pelts, drifted swiftly by on the current. Long narrow keelboats, pointed at each end, were guided by river men walking along the narrow decks with long poles to propel them upstream. Heavy oars, or sweeps mounted at the stern, steered the crafts. Several times the keelboat men blew horns to signal their presence among the river traffic.

"Keelboats can go upstream because they're built long and narrow and don't draw much water," Nancy informed them. "Pa said some of the larger barges can carry passengers downstream from Pittsburgh all the way to New Orleans."

"Look at that boat!" John cried suddenly, forgetting for the moment his worries about finding Mother. "There's a little house on it and a pen full of pigs, all floating down the river."

He was pointing to a boat shaped like a huge raft, with a cabin at one end of it. The cabin even had a fireplace and windows. At the other end was a stock pen for animals.

124

"That's a flatboat," Nancy explained. "They're big clumsy things and always travel downstream with the current. See that steering oar in the back. That's how it's guided. Folks settling down along the Ohio River in Cincinnati or Kentucky travel that way. Pa says most settlers sell their wagons in Pittsburgh to pay for their boats. They can live on the flatboats for days and days and there's enough room to carry their animals."

"They need to be careful of river pirates, though," Freddie piped up, his eyes wide.

"River pirates?" exclaimed John. "I thought pirates were found only at sea."

"Oh, lots of robbers live in caves along the Ohio," Nancy explained. "Pa says it's dangerous for boats to pass their caves at night."

After they grew tired of watching the river, Nancy led the way up Market Street to Thomas Perkins' store.

"Let's go inside and see all the things," she suggested, leading the way into the store.

James and John had never seen so many different things sold in one place before. All kinds of yard goods were for sale: broadcloths, silks, muslins, calicoes, corduroys, chintzes, and linens. There were mantuas for the ladies and hats for the gentlemen. There were toothbrushes and combs and shaving boxes and flints and gunpowder. There were boots and shoes and quills and saddles and frying pans. They stepped up to the counter and sniffed with delight the spices from the Orient. Freddie looked longingly at the chocolate and molasses candies, and James wished he had some money to buy the little boy a treat.

John had his eye on a jew's harp. He remembered

the funny twanging sound it made when a jolly sailor played one at The Ship's Anchor. It looked like fun to play. He sighed and wished he could buy one.

He stuck his hand into his bosom pocket and the next moment his face broke into smiles as his fingertips touched the coins Mrs. Jenkins had given them. He had brought the money all the way across the mountains and had forgotten all about it until now. He brought out the coins and laid them on the counter.

"Let's each buy something," he said generously.

Nancy's eyes grew round when she saw the coins and Freddie hopped up and down on one foot and pointed to the molasses candy.

"Sure, let's buy something," James agreed. He chose some candy, too, and Nancy picked out a string of colored beads. There were enough coins left for John's jew's harp.

Happy with their treasures, the children said goodbye to Thomas Perkins and left the store.

"What do you want to do now?" asked Nancy, glancing down to admire her beads.

"Lets go to the Point," James suggested. "I'd like to stand right on the spot where the three rivers meet."

They walked west on Third Street, past the blockhouse of old Fort Pitt, which was now changed into a dwelling. A little farther on they came to the end of the Point where forty-five years before the French fort, Duquesne, had commanded the three rivers.

"Aye, what a view!" exclaimed James as he walked out on the tip of land where the three rivers meet and looked up at the broad sweep of the Ohio. The western shore of the river was lined with high river bluffs. The steep bluff directly across from the Point, Nancy informed them, was called Coal Hill. To the north of the Point lay Smoky Island where the Indians used to camp during the French and Indian War.

They walked around the Point for awhile and explored the deserted bastions of old Fort Pitt. Then Freddie said to his sister, "Let's show them Fort Fayette. That's a real fort."

So they made their way along the southeast shore of the Allegheny and turned up Penn Street. Ten blocks away on Hand Street they came to the garrison. The gate was open and the sentry standing idly on duty welcomed their company. He let them step inside the stockade to have a look around. James and John stared curiously at the tall log palisades and the four bastions, one in each corner.

The guard pointed out the two blockhouses, one built in the bastion pointing north toward the river and the other in the bastion pointing toward the town. They were studded with loopholes where rifles could be thrust through to fire at approaching enemies. The log barracks for the soldiers stood along the Allegheny River side of the fort and the officers' quarters were directly across from them. The flag of the United States fluttered in a stiff breeze off the river from the flagstaff in the southeast bastion.

"This fort was built for General Anthony Wayne's army and it was from here that the general and his men marched to their last Indian battle," the guard told the boys. "At the Battle of Fallen Timbers in the Ohio country, General Wayne defeated Red Pole and his Indian tribe in the summer of 1794. That battle freed the frontier of Indian raids."

"Do Indians live around here now?" asked John.

The guard nodded. "There are some villages to the north, but the Indians are peaceful since the Battle of Fallen Timbers. That's why more and more easterners are coming to settle here in the western country."

After thanking the guard for showing them around, they left the fort and started down Hand Street.

"Let's go back and see if Mr. Tom has discovered anything at the courthouse," James said anxiously.

"All right," Nancy agreed. "We'll take a short cut down Market Street."

They passed the public square, called the Diamond, and the new courthouse that had been constructed only a year ago. When they arrived at the log house on Third Street, Ada Evans greeted them with some ginger cookies she had just taken from the oven.

"No, lads, my brother isn't home yet," she told them. "But never fear. If your mother's in Pittsburgh, Tom will find her."

"I know he will," James said as he nibbled one of Mrs. Evans's ginger cookies. But just the same, James wished that he could be doing something himself to help find their mother besides just sitting and eating cookies.

Freddie asked if they could spend the rest of the day fishing at Hogg's Pond, and Mrs. Evans thought that was a good idea.

"My Abner says there's no better way to take your mind off your worries than fishing," she said, smiling over at James and John. "The poles are in back of the cabin and I'll pack you a bite to eat to take along."

Hogg's Pond stretched for six blocks below Grant's Hill on the eastern edge of the city. It was a long narrow pond surrounded by cattails and swamp grass.

Nancy said it was a good place to fish for bullheads, and the boys proved her right by bringing home seven large, whiskered fish for supper that night.

Mr. Tom had returned home before them, and one look at his face told the children that he had discouraging news. Not until there were seated around the fire after supper did the circuit rider tell James and John what he had learned that day. He had asked around town for the whereabouts of their mother, but nobody he had talked with remembered ever seeing her in Pittsburgh.

"I inquired at the courthouse about Malcolm McPherson and his claim," he said, "and I fear I have further bad news. Mr. McPherson took sick with lung disease a year ago and died. His wife sold their claim and took her family back East."

"Sold their claim!" exclaimed James. "Then our land is gone, too!"

"It seems that way," Mr. Tom said gravely.

"Maybe when Mother found that out, she went back East, too, Jamie," John suggested, his face clouded with worry.

James raised his head and looked straight at his brother. "I don't think she would do that," he said with conviction. "Father wanted us to settle here in the Ohio Valley. Don't you remember she promised him that we would before he died?"

"Well, then she must be hereabouts, somewhere," Abner Evans spoke up. "We won't give up searching for her yet, lads."

That night before he went to sleep in the attic loft, James opened the precious linen bundle he had carried over the mountains. The six silver spoons glimmered in the moonlight that crept through the little window in the loft. He would never forget the look of pride on Mother's face and the way her blue eyes lighted up when she wrapped the spoons in the linen cloth that day in Ireland before they had left for America.

As he lay back on his straw pallet, troublesome thoughts kept whirling about in his mind. Where could Mother be now, he wondered. Had something happened to her on the way over the mountains? Was that why they had never received her letter from Pittsburgh?

James tossed and turned on his pallet. This was the hardest part of the journey, he thought with sinking heart. Oh, he'd be willing to go through the difficult climb over Sideling Hill, the forest fire, and everything else they had had to endure to get here again, if only at the end of the journey Mother would be here waiting for them.

Sick with worry, he rolled over and buried his face in his pillow so that John wouldn't wake and hear him crying.

Why did they have to leave Ireland for this strange, faraway place, he kept asking himself. If they had stayed in Ireland, Father would be alive now and Mother would be with them as always.

But when he thought of the better life Father had wanted for them in America and how he had given his life for that dream, James felt suddenly ashamed that he had had such thoughts.

He choked back the sobs and wiped the tears from his cheeks. If they could only find Mother, he was sure that everything would be all right again.

THE VENANGO TRAIL

ALMOST A WEEK had passed since James and John
had arrived in Pittsburgh and still there was no word
about their mother. Mr. Tom had asked about her in
the town's taverns, in the stores, at the two churches,
and along the rivers where the boatmen gathered. He
had even put an ad about her in the *Pittsburgh
Gazette*, the town's newspaper. But nobody knew the
whereabouts of a woman named Mary Graham.

John was more discouraged than ever and James,
who had refused to give up hope, was himself beginning to wonder if they'd ever find Mother. It was at
the end of the week, while they were sitting in the little parlor of the Evans's home after supper, that a

knock sounded on the door. Abner arose to answer it and led a young man dressed in a long buckskin tunic and riding boots into the parlor. The man had fiery red hair and a pleasant, boyish smile.

"Why, hello, Mike Higgins," greeted Ada Evans. "Are you back from your latest brave run over the mountains?"

"Aye, that I am, mum," the young Irishman replied. "And I have a bit o' news y' might be wantin'."

"Come sit down, Mike, and I'll get you a cup of tea," Ada said, leading the post rider to the settle by the fire. She reached into the cupboard for her flowered china teapot that she saved for company and while they waited for the tea to brew, Mike Higgins told the purpose of his visit.

"At the post office I heard, Mr. Tom, that y' have been askin' about a Mary Graham, these two lads' mother."

Mr. Tom nodded, leaning forward in his chair, and James and John gathered closer to the post rider to hear what he had to say.

"Well, now, 'twas Mary Graham, herself, I was speakin' to this spring," said Mike Higgins. "I remember her because of how anxious she was to get her letter off to Philadelphia. I was just startin' my eastern run over the mountains and was on my way to my horse with the mailbags when out of the post office she comes hurryin' and asks me to take her letter. She told me she wanted to put the letter into my hands herself so that she'd be sure it got there safely. She said her name was Mary Graham and that she had two lads livin' in Philadelphia."

"Then Mother did write to us!" exclaimed John.

James looked baffled. "But we never got her letter!"

The post rider ran his fingers through his bright red hair and his jolly-looking face turned sober. "I brought the letter to the post office in Philadelphia, lads. I'm sure o' that."

They sat in deep thought for a moment, then Mr. Tom spoke up, as puzzled as James. "If Mary Graham is in Pittsburgh, why can't we find her?"

"I was comin' to that," replied Mike Higgins. "When she gave me the letter, she said she wanted to get it off to her two lads before she left for the Shenango Valley with a man she was keepin' house for and the settlers he was travelin' with."

"The Shenango Valley!" exclaimed John. "Then she's not here in Pittsburgh after all!"

"Where is the Shenango Valley, sir, and how can we get there?" asked James, a look of hope shining in his eyes at the thought that now, at least, they knew where Mother was.

"Faith, it's a long way from Pittsburgh, lad. It's one of the new settlements northwest o'here," replied Mike Higgins, "and there's no way gettin' there that I know of except by pack animals. There's not even a wagon road. Think o' that, now!"

James's hopeful expression faded and the boys looked at one another with concern in their eyes. For a moment nobody had anything to say. Then Mr. Tom broke the silence.

"I've heard tell the Shenango Valley is being settled by a colony from Westmoreland County," he said thoughtfully. "And coming from Westmoreland County, they'd be good, God-fearing people."

Ada Evans glanced at her brother and smiled know-

133

ingly. "They would welcome a circuit rider if one should come their way, Tom."

Mr. Tom nodded, his bright eyes twinkling under the dark brows. "I've never been as far as the Shenango Valley. They say it's a real wilderness up there. With no churches, the settlers will be wondering when the circuit rider will be coming along. I think I ought to ride up there and James and John can ride along with me."

There was a whoop of happy laughter from the children. John was so excited over Mr. Tom's words that he grabbed Nancy by the hand and they did a little jig in front of their laughing elders.

Mr. Tom turned to the post rider. "Did Mary Graham say the name of the man she was working for?"

Mike Higgins sat for a moment, thinking. "Aye, that she did, but I can't remember the name." Then he added in his good-natured way, "But I reckon when ye get to Shenango, ye'll be able to find out easy enough. The settlement's small and everybody's sure to know everybody else."

James looked up at the circuit rider, his heart full of joy. "When will we be leaving, Mr. Tom?"

"As soon as we can get supplies and the horses ready," replied Mr. Tom. "I'd say in a day or two."

That night James and John went to bed happier than they had been in a long time, and the next couple of days they did everything they could to help Mr. Tom get ready for the journey.

Nancy and Freddie helped, too. While the children were running an errand for Mr. Tom, Nancy said, "We heard tell that up north the trees are so big they shut out the sun and the forest is as dark as night in the day." She gave a delightful shiver. "And there's wolves and mountain lions and Indians galore. Wish I was going with you."

"Me too," chimed in Freddie, not wanting to seem less adventuresome than his sister.

The brothers grinned back at the girl and her small brother. They didn't care how big the trees were and how many wolves and mountain lions and Indians they'd see. They just wanted to find Mother.

At last they were ready to leave. The two grays who had hauled the wagon over the mountains from Philadelphia were now transformed into pack horses. Mr. Tom said the boys could ride Joshua. Job, the good and patient follower, would carry the supplies. The boys didn't have much of their own to take. They wrapped their old clothes in their blanket rolls to be strapped on the packsaddle along with Mr. Tom's two saddlebags, one containing the Bibles and hymnbooks from Philadelphia and the other filled with supplies. James put the six silver spoons inside the bosom pocket of his deerskin shirt and reminded John to be sure he had the folding knife.

Mr. Evans shook hands with the boys before they started and wished them a good journey. James thanked the Evanses for their hospitality and Ada gave both boys a kiss. "I do hope you'll find your mother this time," she told them.

Nancy and Freddie said their sober farewells, and even Mike Higgins came to see them off.

James and John mounted Joshua, then Mr. Tom took hold of the lead strap and said, "Come along,

Job." They waved their last good-bye and started up Market Street toward the Allegheny River.

As they crossed over on the ferry, James took his stand beside the bridle of the lead horse and looked back at the town in the forks. On the hills above Pittsburgh the sun was shining warm and bright, but the Point was still shrouded with the usual early morning fog that hung over the three rivers. The faint outlines of the streets and houses looked dim and far away. Pittsburgh would be the last town they would see for a long while, James thought. Now ahead lay what Nancy had called the wilderness.

They left the ferry and followed the Franklin Road along the river. At Pine Creek the road dwindled into a narrow trail that climbed out of the river valley through deep gorges. When they stopped by a spring to water the horses at midday, they met a traveling herb peddler resting underneath a large chestnut tree.

The peddler was dressed in buckskins and wore a coonskin cap with a long pheasant feather fastened rakishly on one side of it. He had a stubby white beard and a lined, weather-beaten face that made him look older than he was.

When they were ready to start out again, he leaped to his feet, as agile as a young man, and called out, "My name's Abraham Jolly. Mind if I join you? It gets mighty lonesome traveling alone."

"We'll be glad for your company," Mr. Tom said. "Where are you going?"

"Up to the settlement along the Connoquenessing Creek," Mr. Jolly replied as his horse fell into step behind Joshua. "Since five years ago settlers have been flocking up there from the counties to the south.

136

Makes business brisk. Before then nobody came this way except frontier scouts and traders and trappers."

"Why was that?" asked John.

"Indians!" exclaimed Mr. Jolly. "All this was Indian country and the Senecas and Delawares were determined that no white man should settle here." He paused and clucked to his horse. "Ever hear the story of Massy Harbison?"

The boys shook their heads and Mr. Tom explained that James and John had just come over from Ireland and this country was new to them.

"Well, 'twas back in '92 that Massy Harbison was captured by the Indians," the talkative peddler went on. "The Harbisons lived only two hundred yards from a blockhouse on the east bank of the Allegheny. Reed's Blockhouse, it was called. Massy's husband was an Indian scout for the blockhouse. Well, one Sunday morning while he was away, the Indians attacked the cabin while Massy was sleeping. They dragged her and her baby with them way up into the northern woods. They traveled day after day, but one night when her guard fell asleep, Massy Harbison escaped with her baby and traveled five days alone in the rain until she reached the blockhouse. She was so thin and weather-beaten that at first nobody recognized her."

James remembered the friendly Indians at Shawnee Cabins. "The Indians around here must be different from the ones we saw crossing the mountains."

"Oh, the Indians living here are friendly now, too," replied Mr. Jolly. "Since the Battle of Fallen Timbers and the Treaty of Greenville in '95, they've ceded all this land to the United States. Nowdays you often see them helping settlers build cabins and barns and they sell them meat and hides. I hear tell they're the best hunters around."

As they rode along, Mr. Tom told the boys that the Indians had made the trail they were following. "It's called the Old Venango Indian Trail and leads from Pittsburgh to Lake Erie. French and English soldiers traveled this trail, and in 1753 young Colonel George Washington used it when he was sent on a mission to French Fort LeBoeuf by the governor of Virginia. It's the only overland route to the north."

Mr. Jolly nodded. "The first trails into the wilderness were deer and bear traces that led to springs and salt licks. Later Indians used these traces, extending them and making them into trails. Now settlers use the Indian trails, branching them off here and there to their settlements. And someday soon these trails will be wagon roads."

James looked around the dense forest they were passing through and wondered how any road could possibly be built through it. As Nancy had said, the trees were so big and tall that they shut out the sun and made the forest seem almost as dim as night. It was a relief when they came out to a natural meadow where the sun was shining brightly. They paused awhile to let the horses graze.

Mr. Jolly reached onto his saddlebag and drew out a large curved horn. "The Indians declare that these meadows used to be filled with elk and buffalo, but there are few of them around now." He held out the horn for the boys to see. "This here's a buffalo horn that was found in these parts by a settler. Traded it for some of my herbs."

John ran his fingers over the smooth curved horn.

He had never seen such a large animal horn as this one. "I'd sure like to see a buffalo," he said. "They must be big animals by the size of this horn."

"They are big," replied Mr. Jolly. "Big and ugly with that hump of theirs. But their hides make good warm robes and that hump meat is good eating. Some settlers even use their wool for spinning when they have no sheep. It's hard to keep a flock of sheep here with so many wild critters around."

The peddler put the buffalo horn to his mouth and blew through the black tip. The high, sharp notes that came from it echoed across the clearing. John reached into his bosom pocket and brought out his jew's harp. He put it to his lips and twanged several notes along with Mr. Jolly's horn call.

The peddler laughed and said, "Well now, lad, between the two of us we do make sweet music!"

They were glad they had met the jolly herb peddler and that he was traveling with them. His tales and jovial company made the hard day's journey seem shorter. When darkness fell over the forest at the end of day, their camp didn't seem so lonely with the peddler there, giving his advice and telling his stories.

Before they bedded down for the night, Mr. Tom asked him if he had ever been as far north as the Shenango Valley.

The peddler shook his head. "I've never been farther north than the Connoquenessing settlement," he said. "But I know how you can get someone to guide you to the Shenango. Just follow this trail until you get to Slippery Rock Creek. Bear west along the creek until you come to Cushcushking, the Seneca Indian village. The Indians there belong to Chief Cornplanter's tribe and a few of them speak English. They're friendly to white travelers and for a few trinkets one of the braves will guide you to the Shenango Valley."

"We'll be glad to have an Indian guide," Mr. Tom said, "but I'll give him more than a few trinkets." He patted the saddlebag that held the Bibles. "I'll give him the Word of God."

In the gray light of dawn the next morning, they were on the trail again. In the deep forest the trail became narrow and difficult to make out at times. Once Job almost stepped into a black pit and Mr. Tom jerked the lead rein just in time.

"Better keep an eye open for those coal pits," Mr. Jolly warned. "Some folks don't care where they dig the black rock out of the ground to burn in their grates."

In the middle of the day they stopped in a small clearing to rest the horses. Some of the large trees surrounding the grassy clearing were charred and James wondered why.

"This used to be an Indian camp," Mr. Jolly explained. "The forest hereabouts is so thick that to make a clearing the Indians have to burn the trees."

John was hot and tired and flung himself down on a flat rock in the shade of one of the charred trees to rest. There didn't seem to be a breath of air stirring. The leaves hung limp and still. There wasn't a sound anywhere, not even a bird call.

John froze with fright and held his breath. The simple motion of breathing might cause the snake to bare its fangs and strike with lightning quick motion.

John stretched out on the cool rock. Suddenly, he heard a dry, buzzing rattle right beside him. He peered down and a sharp sting of terror raced along his spine as he stared at a large, diamond-headed snake, lying in deadly coil. The tail of the snake was waving back and forth, and the rattles on the end of it sounded terrifying in the quiet of the clearing. The rattler was so close that John could see its tiny black eyes.

"Don't move, John!" commanded Mr. Tom in a low, urgent voice. "Nobody move!"

John froze with fright and held his breath lest the simple motion of breathing might cause the snake to bare its fangs and strike with lightning quick motion.

For several long moments the boy lay paralyzed. Then to his horror, the creature uncoiled itself and began to crawl over his body. It was all John could do to stay still as the ugly thing slithered slowly over him. But he knew he couldn't as much as lift a little finger. He didn't dare blink. He hardly dared to breathe, for fear the snake would strike with its deadly fangs.

It seemed like hours later when the snake, in fluid motion, disappeared into the tall grass on the other side of the rock. For another long moment the boy remained rigid with fear.

When they were sure the danger was past and Mr. Tom told John he could get up, the boy leaped off the rock.

Mr. Jolly took off his coonskin cap and wiped his forehead with shaking hands. "Ach, that was a big varmint. Must have been five feet long."

James threw his arms around his brother and held him close for a long moment.

"Oh, Johnny, I was sure the snake would bite you

142

when he crawled over you like that!"

"So was I," exclaimed John, still trembling from the experience.

"Well, rattlesnakes have one noble characteristic," Mr. Tom told them with a shaky laugh. "They will not attack anything they think is dead or is powerless to get away. Many folks have been saved from snakebite because they were too frightened to move."

"I should have warned you lads to be careful hereabouts," Mr. Jolly said, shaking his head. "This country's full of rattlers. I recall the story about a settler's wife in these parts who was out picking blackberries that grew along a rocky bank. She had to climb a dogwood tree because in no time at all, she was surrounded by snakes. She cried out for help but there were so many rattlers around that tree that her husband couldn't chase them off by himself. Had to get his neighbors to help him. With long hickory poles they were able to cut their way through the rattlers to rescue the woman. They say they counted two hundred poisonous snakes that had crawled out of those rocks."

After the encounter with the rattlesnake, they were anxious to be on their way again. For the rest of the day they traveled along the dim trail with a grim determination to stay clear of rocks and fallen logs.

Late in the afternoon they forded a stream and stopped on the other side to camp for the night. They were sitting around the fire, listening to the sad complaint of a whippoorwill in a tree nearby, when John looked up suddenly and exclaimed, "Listen! Isn't that a cowbell?"

They sat quietly for a moment, straining their ears.

The whippoorwill ceased its complaining and Mr. Tom said, "I hear it now, too. It is a cowbell. We must be camped near a settler's clearing."

Mr. Jolly, who was squatting near the fire with his elbows resting on his knees and his hands hanging limp in front of him, nodded and said, "The sweetest of all woodland sounds is the music of a cowbell. But when the Indians were on the rampage around here, a settler had to be mighty careful about cowbells."

"What do you mean?" asked James. "What did Indians have to do with cowbells?"

Mr. Jolly stroked his grizzled beard and they knew that he was about to launch into another one of his stories. "Well, you see, it was a trick Indians used to lure settlers into the woods so they could capture them. They'd take the bell off the cow and hide in the woods with it. When the settler came hunting for his stray cow, the Indian would ring the bell and capture him. I heard tell of quite a number of children being captured that way while they were in the woods looking for stray stock. Of course, now that the Indians are peaceful, it's safe enough to follow a cowbell. Tomorrow we'll find out who that bell belongs to."

And shortly after they were on the trail the next morning, they came to a small clearing. The stumps were still white from the trees that had been recently cut. In the center of the clearing stood a half-faced cabin built of poles and bark that the settler had thrown up for his family to live in until he finished their regular cabin. A big log lay in front of the open side of the shelter against which a fire was kindled. A woman was stirring breakfast in a large kettle over the fire. Several small children were playing in the sun.

144

When the man saw them, he threw his ax into a log and called out, "Ho, strangers! Where you bound?"

"For the Connoquenessing Creek settlement," Mr. Jolly called back.

"Well, you're almost there," the settler said. "We plan on goin' up there to meetin' tomorrow. Got no preacher but we still meet in Adam Brown's pine grove every Sabbath."

"You'll have a preacher tomorrow," Mr. Tom told him.

The settler walked over to the circuit rider and shook his hand. "'Twill pleasure us mightily if you give us a service," he said. "I'll tell my woman. She'll be looking forward to hearing a real preacher tell the sermon."

When they were on their way again, Mr. Tom said cheerfully, "Well, lads, tonight we'll have a roof over our heads. Adam Brown has a nice dry barn and will be glad to put us up. I've slept there before when I preached at the settlement."

The boys were as happy as Mr. Tom with the prospects of spending the night in the Connoquenessing Creek settlement. They looked forward to sleeping with a roof over their heads again and eating a meal cooked by a woman. Mr. Tom's cooking was all right, but they were getting tired of johnnycake and jerky at every meal.

John gave Joshua a pat on the rump to hurry him along. "Come on, horse," he called happily. "Get a move on or we'll never get there."

SERMON IN THE PINES

ADAM BROWN'S cabin was even more primitive than the Wrights' cabin at Sideling Hill. It was a rude log building erected in the midst of the big trees of the forest. The logs were hand-hewn and notched at the ends to fit together, the cracks between them chinked with mud and straw to keep out the cold winter wind. Above the clapboard roof, a mud and stick chimney sent forth a welcoming feather of smoke.

Mr. Tom walked up to the door and knocked. He waited several moments. "Nobody's home right now," he said, "but the latchstring's out." He pulled on the buckskin cord that dangled through a small hole, and the heavy door of hewn puncheons swung open on its wooden hinges. The boys and Mr. Jolly followed him inside.

"There's a fresh fire on the grate," observed Mr. Jolly, "so they can't be far." He looked around at the wooden pegs inserted in the walls where the clothing was hung—a deerskin hunting shirt, a woman's woolen shawl, shirts of linsey-woolsey, and a straw hat.

"We'll sit down and wait for them," Mr. Tom said, walking over to the wooden settle alongside the fire.

They didn't have long to wait, for a barking dog and footsteps announced the return of the occupant. The latchstring was pulled, lifting the wooden bar on the inside, and the door opened. A tall, spare woman with a split-oak basket on her arm entered the cabin. When she saw them sitting there, she called out, "Well, now, howdy. I saw your horses outside and knew it must be the circuit rider and the herb peddler. I'm right glad you made yourselves at home."

She put her basket on the table. "My dog and I been gathering berries down by the spring and my man went to the gristmill to get our grain and our neighbor's ground. He won't be back till sundown."

Mr. Tom stood up and smiled at the woman. "I'll be glad to do some preaching tomorrow for you folks."

The woman's thin, sallow face wrinkled up with pleasure. "You know you're right welcome here in the settlement, Mr. Tom," she said. "You can all bed down in the barn. It's warm and dry this time of year. Now I'll just get busy and stir up some fixin's for supper. My man sure will be anxious to hear the news you bring from Pittsburgh." And she scurried around the little cabin like a busy bee around a hive.

For the rest of the day they helped her with her

147

chores. James and John carried water from the spring and picked greens and vegetables from the garden patch. Mr. Tom and Mr. Jolly chopped enough firewood to fill the large woodbox by the hearth. By the time their chores were done, Mr. Brown drove his team of two chestnut-brown horses into the clearing.

The horses were hitched to a queer-looking contraption that looked more like a big wooden sled than a wagon. Two long, sturdy, wooden runners were attached to the flat wagon bed on which were piled several sacks of ground flour.

As the boys helped unload the sacks and put them into the barn, John asked curiously, "Why don't you have wheels on your wagon, Mr. Brown?"

The settler gave a hearty laugh and explained, "Till we get decent roads around here, we have to use runners instead of wheels, laddie. Wheels wouldn't go over our rough trails, but a sled will go over most anything—through mud and snowdrifts, over rocks and stumps."

At that moment Mrs. Brown came to the door and called for supper. James and John groaned with delight when they saw all the food on the rude split-log table. On a large wooden trencher was a golden brown turkey that Mr. Brown had shot the day before. Next to it were bowls of succotash, greens from the garden, turnips, and fresh baked corn pone with a comb of wild honey and steaming noggins of sassafras tea.

They all ate heartily. After supper while the boys were helping Mrs. Brown clear the table, Mr. Tom opened his saddlebag and brought out one of his new Bibles, a hymnbook, and a copy of the *Pittsburgh Gazette*.

"I thought you might want to read about what's happening in Pittsburgh and back East," he said, handing Mr. Brown the paper.

"I thank you," the settler replied as he held the paper toward the firelight to read the headlines.

"And ma'am," Mr. Tom continued, "the last time I was here you mentioned that you had lost your Bible on your way to Pennsylvania from Virginia. I'll leave this one with you and a hymnbook for your meetings."

Mrs. Brown's eyes lighted up as she took the Bible and hymnbook. Then both Mr. Tom and Mr. Jolly talked about the happenings in Pittsburgh and the stream of pioneers who were opening new settlements along the Ohio River and to the north.

"The back country's growing fast," Mr. Jolly said with a note of pride in his voice. "I'll wager soon Pittsburgh will be a big city, like the ones in the East."

They talked until the fire in the grate grew to red coals. Then Mrs. Brown handed Mr. Tom her new Bible and asked him to read some Scripture. Later when the boys lay down in the sweet-smelling hay in the barn, they thought they had never had such good beds. There were no wolves lurking nearby and no panthers screaming frightful cries through the dark trees to keep them awake that night. They rolled up in their blankets and were soon asleep.

The Sabbath dawned bright and clear. The August sky was a deep blue and the pines in the grove murmured softly in a gentle breeze. In one of the tall trees a happy song sparrow heralded the new day with clear, sweet notes.

"Listen to that chippy," John told James as he

searched the branches of the pine for the gay chorister.

The little grove of pines next to Amos Brown's cabin was filling with neighboring settlers who had come from far and near to hear the circuit rider from Pittsburgh. The men sat on logs and the women on rough-hewn benches between the trees. Amos Brown had fashioned an altar from a large pine trunk. Mr. Tom stood behind it to conduct the prayer meeting and preach the sermon. A hush fell over the congregation as Mr. Tom opened the service by reading Psalm 121:

I will lift up mine eyes unto the hills, from whence cometh my help.
My help cometh from the Lord, which made heaven and earth.
He will not suffer thy foot to be moved: he that keepeth thee will not slumber.
Behold, he that keepth Israel shall neither slumber nor sleep.
The Lord is thy keeper: the Lord is thy shade upon thy right hand.
The sun shall not smite thee by day, nor the moon by night.
The Lord shall preserve thee from all evil: he shall preserve thy soul.
The Lord shall preserve thy going out and thy coming in from this time forth, and even for evermore.

As he listened to the words of the familiar old psalm, James thought about David, the shepherd boy, on a lonely hillside in Judea, watching his sheep. He, too, had been in the wilderness, but he had put his faith in the Lord and the Lord had not failed him.

After the psalm was read, a young man in the

150

gathering arose and led the congregation in the singing of Psalm 100 to the tune of "Old Hundred." The swelling harmony from these sturdy pioneer voices filled James with a thrill he had never experienced within the walls of the little kirk in Ireland. Surrounded by the beauties of God's earth and sky, it was no wonder that these simple men and women praised the Creator with such lusty voices.

After the singing, it was time for prayer. Amos Brown arose first and after him several other settlers stood and poured out the hopes and fears, the sorrows and the thankfulness of a pioneering people.

The prayer meeting over, a breath of expectancy passed through the gathering as Mr. Tom arose once more to take his stand by the pine trunk altar. His sermon was as comforting a message to the people of the back country as the psalm of David he had read during the prayer meeting. He preached with a sincerity and earnestness that obviously made a deep and lasting impression on the listeners. He spoke of David's God, a God of love and help in times of trial. He assured the congregation that the sick and weary and sorrowing would find comfort in heaven if they remained faithful to God on earth. And when he ended by describing the glories of heaven, a chorus of "Amen!" "Hallelujah!" and "Praise the Lord!" rose from the entire congregation.

At midday the food the women had prepared was eaten in the shade of the pines. When the meal was over and the men and boys had fed and watered the horses, the settlers assembled for the afternoon session. Several children were taught from the catechism and there was more singing and praying. Then all heads were bowed for the benediction.

It was the middle of the afternoon before the settlers made preparations for departing. Renewed with the love of God which would give them courage in the hard days to come, they shook Mr. Tom's hand and said their good-byes with full hearts.

Down the narrow, shadowy trail they went, some singing the words of "Old Hundred" in the same spirited way they had sung at the meeting.

As James and John watched the departing horses and listened to the voices becoming dimmer through the deep gloom of the forest, they knew that they would never forget this bright Sabbath day and the simple sermon in the pines.

CUSHCUSHKING

THEY missed Mr. Jolly and his stories the next day as they journeyed northward along the Venango Trail. The peddler had stayed behind in the Connoquenessing colony to sell his herbs to the settlers. When they said good-bye, he had given the brothers each a small bunch of dried peppermint leaves. "It makes dandy-tasting tea," he told them, "and is good for the belly-ache."

For two days they traveled along the Venango Trail, following it northward toward Slippery Rock Creek.

"You can't miss that creek," Mr. Jolly had told them. "You'll know it by its rocks and boulders. I heard tell it has more rocks than water."

"And there's a tommyhawk mark cut into the trunk of a big ash tree on the northern bank of the creek," Amos Brown had added. "A trapper who was up there last fall said it's an Indian blaze showin' the trail to the Cushcushking village. Follow the creek westward until it branches into Wolf Creek and there you'll find the Senecas."

North of the Connoquenessing settlement the trail had become less steep and winding. It had leveled out over high, rolling land, dipping occasionally into gentle valleys. Along the way they crossed many creeks and streams, but they knew at once when they had come to Slippery Rock Creek.

As they stood along the bank and viewed the mass of rocks and boulders that were strewn in the creek bed, James remarked, "I can see now why it's called Slippery Rock."

"The French soldiers from Fort Machault named it that," Mr. Tom told them. "The fort was just north of here, but it was destroyed in 1759 during the French and Indian War."

With a critical eye the circuit rider viewed the swift water swirling around the moss-covered boulder he squatted on. Lichens and damp moss coated the surface of most of the rocks to make the footing treacherous. He knew they couldn't expect the horses to cross over these slippery rocks without falling. Surely there must be a channel somewhere where the Senecas and white trappers forded the creek.

"I'll walk down this way and look for a crossing," he told the boys. "You can walk up along the bank in the other direction."

They tied the horses to some sturdy saplings and

started reconnoitering. As Mr. Jolly had said, there seemed to be more rocks than water.

John laughed. "I wonder if some giant in prehistoric times had fun tossing these rocks into this creek."

"Aye, it would seem that way if there were such things as giants," his brother replied, "but Mr. Tom said it was the glacier during the Ice Age that left all these rocks around here."

He stopped talking and pointed to a watery pathway between several flat boulders. "Do you think it's wide enough to get the horses through?"

"Aye," John replied. "You stay here so we don't have to hunt for the place again and I'll get Mr. Tom."

When John and Mr. Tom returned with the horses, the circuit rider studied the channel carefully. "Let's try it," he said at last.

He took a tight hold of the lead rein and started down the bank of the creek. "Come along, Joshua," he urged, giving the rein a tug.

At the sight of the swirling water, the big gray shied and blew through his muzzle, but Mr. Tom held the bridle strap firmly and urged the horse to step into the swift, rocky stream. The patient Job followed with John leading him.

James was fearful that one of the horses might stumble and go down between the slippery boulders. He held his breath as he watched them slowly and patiently make their way across, the water up to their knees.

"It's good it's August and the creek's low," Mr. Tom called back encouragingly. "If it were spring and the water high, we'd never be able to make it across."

At last they reached the other side and the horses

strained to climb the steep bank. Drawing their great bodies up on dry ground again, they stood stamping their muddy hoofs and shaking their withers.

Mr. Tom patted the flanks of each horse and said, "Good work, Joshua—Job. We made it!" Turning to the boys, he said, "Now let's hunt for that ash tree with the blaze mark and make camp for the night."

James, who had been looking around at the trees along the bank, spied it first. "Is that the tomahawk mark over there?" he asked, pointing to a white gash cut into the dark bark of a big tree.

Mr. Tom looked to where the boy was pointing. "That's an ash all right, so it must be the right one." Several yards from the tree they noticed a well-worn trail leading westward.

They camped by the ash tree that night and the next morning followed the trail westward along Slippery Rock Creek. Toward the end of that day they came to the place where the rocky stream branched northward into Wolf Creek. Beyond some low-hanging tree branches they spied a cluster of bark lodges along the bank of the stream. "Cushcushking Village," Mr. Tom said.

The boys held the horses while the circuit rider walked ahead to inquire about a guide to lead them to the Shenango settlement. While they waited, they looked curiously at the Seneca lodges. Covered with sheets of elm bark, these long lodges had several holes in each roof from which the smoke of cooking fires drifted through. Several families must live in each long-house, James thought.

The lodges stood around a central open space where Indian women were drying meat on wooden racks and pounding corn in stone mortars. Some of the women and girls were working in the gardens and cornfield which stretched along the banks of the creek. Under a shady elm a group of small children were playing a game of fox and geese with corn kernels. The whole scene, James thought, was not much different from any white settlement in the back country.

Mr. Tom appeared with a tall Seneca brave. "This is Running Deer," he said. "He will guide us to the Shenango Valley. He speaks English."

Running Deer's long black hair hung down to his shoulders and his piercing dark eyes seemed to take in everything at once. He held his head proudly and spoke broken English in a soft, dignified voice.

"My father chief," he told the boys. "You welcome to spend night in village. Come, I show where to put horses."

They followed the young brave to a round enclosure where they left Joshua and Job to graze with several Indian ponies. Then Running Deer led them to a small lodge built of squared-up logs and motioned for them to enter.

"This lodge for guests," Running Deer told them. He pointed to the bunks of pine wood along the back wall. "Sleep here."

Mr. Tom put his saddlebags on the top bunk and the boys spread their blankets on a mattress of soft balsam boughs in the lower one. After they were settled, Running Deer showed them around the village. On a small rise of ground behind the lodges, they were surprised to see a circular stockade with a breastwork three feet high and a ditch around it two feet deep. The breastwork had gates on the land side and on the opposite side stretched the dark waters of a swamp.

"I didn't know Indians had forts like white settlers," exclaimed John.

Mr. Tom nodded soberly. "During the Indian wars the Senecas here were in as much danger of attack by white soldiers as white settlers were from Indian warriors. When Running Deer's village was under attack, his people took refuge in this fort. I have heard that there are quite a few Indian forts in these northern forests."

Later when they returned to their lodge, they found a squaw tending a large cook pot which hung over the fire pit in the middle of the ground floor. She ladled out a rabbit stew made with corn and beans and potatoes that tasted every bit as good to the hungry boys as the stews Mr. Tom's sister made. While they ate, they were visited by Running Deer's father, who sat by the fire pit and talked with Mr. Tom.

The chief was a strong, handsome man dressed in a beaded hunting shirt similar to his son's. He wore a necklace of bear claws that showed what a brave and fearless hunter he was. He held his head proudly and was as quick-eyed as Running Deer. In a low and dignified voice, he spoke with a lilting rhythm. He was pleased with the Bible Mr. Tom gave him. When the circuit rider promised that he would return and teach him how to read it, the chief's dark eyes spoke their gratitude.

For a long while the two men talked together and it was well into the night before the chief left their lodge. Exhausted, the boys dropped off to sleep at once.

That night John dreamed about Mother. He dreamed that she was reaching out for him and that he was running toward her. But he could never reach her because she kept drifing away from him.

"Mother!" he called out in his sleep. "Mother, where are you?"

The dream vanished when a comforting hand tucked the blanket closer around him. When John fell into a more peaceful sleep, Mr. Tom smiled down at the boy, then climbed up into his own bunk.

THE SHENANGO VALLEY

AT the first light of dawn, Running Deer was ready to leave. The friendly Senecas came to the lodge to see them off. The chief brought them presents—a large bear robe for Mr. Tom and, to the boys' delight, two owls carved out of soapstone.

On his brown Indian pony, Running Deer led the way out of the village and up Wolf Creek. He rode silently. Before long they realized that, unlike his father, Running Deer was a man of few words.

When the trail rounded a bend, James took a glance back at the Seneca village, but it was already out of sight in the green shadows of the forest. The trail turned and twisted as it followed the creek and seemed little more than an animal trace. They made their way past deep ravines covered with creepers and wild grape-vines and through groves so dense that the tight umbrella of pine boughs overhead scarcely let a ray of light penetrate through to the brown carpet of needles on the forest floor.

Once the forest gave way to a great swamp, a dismal-looking place with gray skeletons of trees protruding from patches of black water. As they skirted the edge of it, James thought, "Here is the forest as God created it, untouched by ax or plow. Without Running Deer to guide us, we would be help-lessly lost." He wondered how Mother and her party of settlers had found their way through this deep woods.

By midday heavy clouds began to sweep over the treetops, making the forest seem as dark as night, and by late afternoon rain began to fall. They stopped early to make camp. Running Deer and Mr. Tom cut several saplings and in a short time built a three-sided lean-to, a shelter of poles covered with thick hemlock boughs that the boys had gathered. Running Deer rolled a big log at the open end of the lean-to against which a fire was kindled and by the time darkness fell, they had a snug shelter with a roaring fire between them and the storm.

Running Deer opened his saddlebag and set out their supper. "Pemmican," he said. "Good food on trail."

John tasted his portion. "What's it made of?" he asked.

"Dried venison pounded in a mortar and mixed with parched corn, maple sugar, and deer tallow," Mr. Tom informed him.

"You like?" asked Running Deer, his dark eyes questioning.

John nodded politely and managed a smile as he rolled the strange-tasting concoction around in his mouth. Mr. Tom boiled some water and filled their drinking horns with peppermint tea to wash down the pemmican.

After their scanty meal, the boys sat quietly, looking out at the gloomy, dripping forest. Beyond their campfire the dark uncertainty of the wilderness pressed in on them like the bars of a prison.

Above the dripping of the rain from the leaves and the groaning of tree branches in the wind, came a high, mournful wail.

"Wolf on the hunt," Running Deer remarked, and the boys shuddered at the eerie sound.

"I know what we can do to shut out the gloomy night," Mr. Tom spoke up.

"What?" they asked anxiously.

"We can sing," the circuit rider suggested, his blue eyes crinkling up in the firelight. "Let's see who can sing the loudest and scare that old wolf away."

"Oh, you can!" said John, laughing. Then remembering his jew's harp, he brought it out and began to twang a merry tune on it. He noticed that Running Deer kept looking curiously at the strange instrument he was playing, and once John saw a quick smile flicker across the young brave's face.

James put another log on the fire and in the rising wind the flames leaped about like a living thing. The stormy night didn't seem so lonely and fearful now as the fire blazed and they joined in with Mr. Tom's lusty singing:

O God, our help in ages past,
Our hope for years to come,
Our shelter from the stormy blast,
And our eternal home. . . .

A wet, gray morning greeted them when they started northward the next day. Wisps of early morning mist curled like long fingers around the black rain-soaked tree trunks. The cold, white dampness seemed to crawl under their buckskin shirts and into their very bones. Even though James was eager to get to the Shenango Valley, he wished they could have built up the fire and warmed themselves before starting out.

The trail led them west and north through thick woods and patches of open glades. Only the cry of a hawk flying overhead broke the silence of the lonely forest. James was glad when the sun came up and burned off the mist.

Toward the end of the day, when they were threading their way across a clearing of tall ryegrass and cedar, they met a man leading a line of pack horses. They stopped to talk with him.

"I'm ridin' south to Pittsburgh to get supplies," the trader told them. "Whereabouts you all headin'?"

"To the Shenango settlement," replied Mr. Tom.

"Well, you'll find the cabins strung out along the Little Shenango River on down to where it joins the Big Shenango," the man said. "It's purty country. You'll be there by tomorrow." He paused and pointed back from where he had come. "The Roberts' cabin is just up the trail from here. They'll be proud to put you up for the night." And with a wave of his hand, he was off down the trail.

A short time later they came to a clearing where they saw a man grinding meal at a hand-mill and a woman sitting on a bench making moccasins. The settlers put aside their work and went eagerly to meet the strangers.

"Not many folks travel this way and you're welcome to stay the night," Mr. Roberts said as he greeted them.

The horses were put out to pasture in a small grassy spot behind the cabin and after a meal of stewed venison and cornbread, they sat around the cheerful hearth to talk.

"Aye, 'twas lonesome country when my wife and I first settled here," Mr. Roberts told them. He smiled over at his wife who had gathered up some flax and was sitting by her spinning wheel. "Elizabeth was the first white woman within twenty miles when we settled here in '97. She sure was a brave woman to follow me back to this wilderness. Why the forest was so dense then that when I was out huntin', she'd stand on the cabin roof and blow the old cowhorn so that I'd be able to find my way home. When I'd hear that horn, I'd shoot off my fowling piece to let her know I was comin'."

Mrs. Roberts looked up from her spinning, nodded, and smiled. While the men continued to talk, James slipped over by her side to watch her spin the nettle flax into strands of long pale thread.

"I wish there was a loom hereabouts to web up this

Running Deer and Mr. Tom cut several saplings and built a three-sided lean-to. They covered the poles with thick hemlock boughs that the boys gathered.

flax into linen cloth," she told the boy. "I got some wool spun, too. My man and boys could use new linsey-woolsey shirts."

"My father was a weaver," James said, "and I want to be one, too."

"Well, we could use weavers in the settlements," Mrs. Roberts told him. "But first you'll have to build yourself a loom."

James didn't know whether or not he could build a loom by himself. He had hoped there would be a weaver somewhere in the Shenango Valley who could show him how.

Above the soft hum of the spinning wheel, they listened to the men talking. Mr. Roberts was telling Mr. Tom and Running Deer about a man and woman in the Shenango Valley who wanted to get married. "They're just waitin' for a preacher to come by," Mr. Roberts said. "Man's name is John Patterson. He's new in the settlement and we don't know much about him 'cept he's a good man and hard worker. Got his cabin built this summer and was even able to put in a late crop."

"When the rider comes around with the weddin' notice, we'll be ready," Mrs. Roberts added with a sparkle in her eye. "There isn't a happier get-together in the settlements than a marryin' and the merriment afterwards."

"And with a preacher headin' there, the marryin' won't be far off, I'll be bound," Mr. Roberts added, winking at the circuit rider.

"We came over the mountains with a family named Patterson," Mr. Tom remarked. "Man's name was David Patterson." In the next breath he asked, "How can we find this John Patterson?"

Mr. Roberts rose to turn the logs in the fire. "Just follow the blazes on the trees borderin' the trail," he replied. "Them blazes will lead you to the Little Shenango River. John Patterson's cabin is near the forks where the Little Shenango joins the Big Shenango. You can't miss it."

The next morning, the last day of their journey, they were all impatient to be off. After Mr. Tom had left the Roberts' one of his Bibles and thanked them for their hospitality, Running Deer prodded his horse and started for the trail. Following the clear ax cuts on the bark of the trees leading westward, they presently came to a wide stream, its banks green with hemlocks.

"Little Shenango," Running Deer said, and James felt an anxious thrill run through him. They had come to the Shenango Valley at last!

All morning they followed the Little Shenango and when it joined the Big Shenango River, they knew they were not far from the settler's cabin. Mr. Tom had told them that when they found John Patterson, he felt sure the settler would be able to locate their mother. Maybe she'd be at the wedding with the other settlers, James thought happily.

A short distance from the forks, Running Deer pointed to a clearing up ahead. The stumps of recently hewn trees were still in the dooryard and beyond them stood a large cabin, its logs still newly yellow and not the weather-beaten brown of older cabins.

As they stopped their horses in the clearing, a dog barked curiously and came running around the corner of the cabin to see who they were. When he saw them, he barked with delight, wagging his tail furiously, his small brown body wiggling with joyous recognition as he danced around the horses.

John stared down at the dog and his heart leaped. He'd know that little brown dog anywhere. But before he could slide off Joshua's back and gather the dog in his arms, a girl came flying out of the cabin.

"Rowdy!" she called. "Rowdy, come here!"

James gasped when he saw the girl's honey-colored hair shining in the sunlight.

"Janey!" he shouted. "Janey Patterson! What are you doing here?"

THE WEDDING

FOR A MOMENT the girl stood speechless with surprise, looking up at them, her blue eyes filled with wonder. Then realizing that what she saw was real, she hopped up and down and cried, "James and John! You've come! You've come, just like you promised!"

The boys slid off Joshua's back and ran to meet her.

"Janey, what are you and Rowdy doing here?" they called, still hardly daring to believe that they were speaking to the same girl they had traveled with over the mountains.

"Mama and I often come over here to visit with Uncle John," Janey explained. "He's helping Papa finish our new cabin."

Mr. Tom tied Joshua and Job to a pine sapling and came over to where they were standing. "So John Patterson is your uncle," he said. "And this is where you folks have settled—in the Shenango Valley!"

Janey bobbed her head up and down. "Our cabin's over yonder across the creek."

"Well, what do you know!" John's voice had a happy ring. "We never thought we'd meet you folks here."

"We had no idea John Patterson could be your uncle," James added, picking up Rowdy in his arms and hugging the squirming little dog.

A woman appeared in the doorway. "Janey, who's there?"

Mr. Tom answered for the girl. "Hello, Mrs. Patterson. It's James and John and Mr. Tom."

The woman fairly flew across the clearing. "Mr. Tom," she cried out joyfully, "and James and John! What a surprise!"

After she had hugged and kissed each one of them, Mr. Tom said, "We understand there's to be a marryin' here. I thought I could be of some service."

"Oh, you can! You can!" exclaimed the woman. "And I'm so happy it's you who came along to do it!"

She stopped short and looked at the boys. There was a strange, excited expression on her face. She turned back to Mr. Tom and it seemed to James that some unspoken message flashed from her eyes for a moment.

Then, in a breathless voice, she said, "My husband is across the creek working in the loft of our new cabin and his brother is in the barn milking. You must come in and—and meet the woman John's going to marry."

She took both boys by the hand and led them up to

the cabin. Mr. Tom stayed behind to help Running Deer take the horses to the barn and Janey followed her mother, with Rowdy running circles around them all, his tail wagging a mile a minute.

A warm cozy light from the hearth inside shone through the cabin window and James noticed that the window had a pane of glass which John Patterson must have brought all the way from Pittsburgh. They entered the cabin and in a quick glance the boys' eyes took in the large pleasant room—the stout puncheon floor swept clean with sand; John Patterson's split-log bed across the end; the long table in the middle, its raw newly hewn logs stained a rich brown with dark walnut hull brew; the ladder that led up to the cozy loft above; and the great fireplace with its array of iron trivets, skillets, crane, and copper pots. It was a fine new cabin and larger than many they had seen in the back country.

But it was the woman bending over a big iron kettle suspended from the pot hook, stirring a savory-smelling stew, that held James's gaze. Her slim body swayed slightly with her stirring motions and the glow from the fire shone on her red hair. She turned to meet the strangers and the firelight was full on her face.

James caught his breath, his heart thumping wildly. What he saw seemed impossible after all this long time, but when the woman let out a surprised gasp and opened her arms to greet them, he knew that their long journey was over at last.

Both boys ran into her arms at once. "Mother! Oh, Mother!" cried John, tears of joy running down his cheeks. "It's you. It's really you!"

"Yes, it's really me!" Mother said breathlessly, half-laughing and half-crying herself.

At the happy reunion Mrs. Patterson took out a handkerchief and wiped her own moist eyes. Janey willingly took over stirring the stew while Mary Graham led her sons to the long settle by the fire where they sat down. She wanted to hear, this very moment, all about them and what had happened after she had left them in Philadelphia.

John still found it hard to believe that Mother was really here, sitting right next to him. He snuggled close and kept squeezing her hand as they told of their adventures.

They told what had happened at The Ship's Anchor, how they had run away in the night and found Mr. Tom, how they had traveled over the mountains with the circuit rider, and how he had helped them find her here in the Shenango Valley.

"Thank God you found such a good and loyal friend to guide you over the mountains," Mother said. Then it was her turn to tell them her adventures. "When I found that Malcolm McPherson had died and that his family had sold their land and returned to the East, I was about to return to Philadelphia myself, but your dear father's words kept haunting me and I remembered my promise to him to make a home for you boys in the Ohio Valley.

"I was fortunate to find work and a home with John Patterson in Pittsburgh," she continued. "His poor wife died last year with the ague and he needed a housekeeper. When he asked me to travel with him and his friends to their claims here in Shenango, I decided to come along."

She stopped for breath. "But before we left this

spring, I sent a letter to you boys. It's strange that you didn't get it and the money I sent for your journey here."

James and John shook their heads and their mother looked puzzled. "I can't understand why you didn't get it. I gave it to the post rider myself, just before he left for the East."

James spoke up grimly, "I've been thinking and thinking about why we didn't get that letter, Mother, and I think I know why now."

John looked at his brother with an expression of quick interest. "Why didn't we get it, Jamie?"

"Because Mr. Jenkins must have got it first and didn't want us to know about it," James replied. "He must have kept the money you sent, Mother, and that's how he found out about the silver spoons."

John nodded soberly. "Aye, that must be what happened."

"Well, thank goodness you got the spoons back to pay for your journey over the mountains," Mother exclaimed.

Before James could tell her that they didn't have to use the spoons to pay for their journey, John asked eagerly, "What did you write in the letter, Mother?"

His mother smiled down at him. "Well, I wrote about my plans for settling here in the Shenango Valley and that when you got to Pittsburgh, you should look up a Mr. Henry Pruitt, the land agent for the Shenango Company, and he would see that you boys got to our settlement.

"But when you didn't come, I began to worry," she continued. "Then David Patterson and his family arrived here, and when they found out I was your mother, they told about you two being in Pittsburgh with the circuit rider. John said that as soon as David's cabin was finished, he would ride to Pittsburgh to fetch you and the circuit rider so that John and I could get married."

"Married!" exclaimed James, his mouth falling open. "Then—then you are the woman John Patterson is going to marry?"

Mother looked at her sons' surprised faces and her voice softened. "Yes, I am the woman John Patterson is going to marry. John is a good man, kind and generous and loving like your father. He needs a wife in this new land and I need a husband and a home for you boys. We have both shared in our sorrow together, and by doing so, have learned to respect and love one another."

She stopped talking and her eyes shone with warmth as she glanced toward the door. James saw the pretty-young-girl look on her face again as she stood up to meet the tall, lean man who stood there with a piggin of milk in his hand.

"John, come and meet my sons," she called out happily.

The man's smiling brown eyes shone with surprise and pleasure as he set the piggin on the table and joined them by the fire.

"So these are the lads I have been hearing so much about!" he said heartily as he shook their hands. "Aye, 'tis good you are here. You will add happiness to our wedding."

Presently Mr. Tom and David Patterson stepped inside the cabin and there was another joyous reunion.

While Mother and Mrs. Patterson dished up the

stew, John Patterson sat down on the settle to get acquainted with his new family. As he listened to the boys' account of their search for their mother, he nodded his head now and then with understanding. James liked this big, friendly man. He liked the soft way he spoke and the gentle tenderness in his eyes when he looked up now and then at their mother.

When they finished telling about their adventures, John Patterson put his strong arms around both of them and said, "I hope I can take James Graham's place and be as good a father to you boys as he has been. I'll surely try," he promised.

Supper that night was a happy affair. Running Deer joined them, sitting at his place at the table in his quiet Indian fashion, his sharp, dark eyes taking in everything. When they invited him to the wedding, which was to be held in two days, he nodded his head that he would stay.

All the next day the cabin by the Shenango River hummed with activity as everybody chipped in to prepare for the wedding. The women baked a large cake, using most of the precious sugar. John Patterson, Running Deer, and Mr. Tom went into the woods to hunt for game for the wedding feast. Mrs. Patterson baked her best and lightest pone and her husband rode through the settlement to spread the happy news to settlers near and far.

The boys and Janey decorated the cabin with wild flowers and evergreens. "Just think, Janey, after Mother gets married to John Patterson, we'll be cousins," James told her, "and we'll see you and Rowdy all the time."

"Then I can pull your braids every day!" John teased happily. And he reached out his hand to give them a playful tug.

Janey ducked her head and tickled John in the face with a hemlock bough. Their playful commotion set Rowdy to barking and running around so excitedly that he almost upset Mrs. Patterson's pans of cooling pone. After that the little dog was sent outside and Mother took a hand in the decorating to keep the children quiet, although she was glad to see John acting like a happy, mischievous boy again.

That afternoon Mother got out her best gray dress from the trunk in the loft and smoothed it with loving hands. "Your father wove the cloth for this dress on his loom in Ireland," she told the boys.

"I wish there was a loom here in the settlement," James said wistfully, "then I'd learn to weave you cloth for another one."

Mother turned to look at him with a smile. "There is a weaver by trade in the settlement," she told him. "And his name is John Patterson."

James' eyes widened with surprise. "*Our* John Patterson?"

Mother laughed and gave him a little squeeze. "Our John Patterson," she replied. "This winter he would like you to help him build a loom like the one he had in Ireland. And he'll teach you to become a weaver, like your father."

James' eyes brightened. "Oh, I'd like that!"

Mother hung her wedding dress on a wooden peg by the open door to allow the wrinkles to blow out, then she helped Mrs. Patterson put a clean cloth on the table which had been lengthened to stretch the entire length of the big cabin room. Mother set out the ironstone plates, the pewter noggins, and the wooden-handled knives. Mrs. Patterson had brought over her good blue delftware meat platter and placed it in the center of the table.

"I wish I had something pretty to go with that lovely platter," Mother said wistfully.

It was then that James remembered the silver spoons. He had carried the precious linen bundle inside his bosom pocket for so long that he had become accustomed to its being there. In the excitement of planning for the wedding, he had completely forgotten it.

His fingers quivered with excitement and happiness as he reached inside his buckskin shirt and drew out the bundle. "You have, Mother," he said, handing her the spoons.

Mary Graham sank down on the settle by the fire and stared at the linen wrapping as if she were afraid to open it.

"Go on, open it!" urged John.

With trembling hands, Mother unwrapped the cloth and there on her lap lay the six silver spoons. Her eyes misted over as she ran her fingers over their shining smooth hardness. "After you told me about Mr. Jenkins taking the traveling money I sent you, I thought I'd never see these spoons again," she said softly, looking up at her sons.

"Mr. Tom wouldn't take them as payment for bringing us to Pittsburgh," James explained. "He said we could help him instead."

"And I hope you did," Mother said.

"Oh, we did," John piped up, remembering the

long, hard climb over Sideling Hill and the fire at the foothills of Allegheny Mountain.

Mrs. Patterson leaned over Mother and picked up one of the spoons. "How lovely!" she breathed. "They must have come from the old country."

"They were given to me by my grandmother in Scotland as a wedding present," Mother replied. "And now they are given to me again as a wedding present by my two sons."

"That's what we want them to be," James spoke up happily. "They are your very special wedding present from us."

Mother arose and hugged the two boys. "I couldn't have asked for a better gift," she told them.

Janey helped lay the silver spoons on the table next to the blue delftware platter. "Now the table really looks beautiful," she murmured.

The children got back to their decorating and by the time the men returned home, the cabin was aglow with a festive look. The hunters had shot plenty of small game and several wild turkeys. "Enough to feed the settlement for a week," exclaimed Mrs. Patterson when she saw all the game.

"Well, the entire settlement's coming to the marrying," her husband informed her, "so it's good we have plenty of food for the wedding feast."

Early the next morning a steady stream of neighbors from near and far came pouring into the new cabin, each with a gift for the bride and groom.

Mrs. Patterson gave Mother a pretty rose-colored china mug to keep the six silver spoons in. Mr. Tom's gift was one of his new hymnbooks. And from his sad-

178

dlebag, Running Deer drew out several beautiful pelts, skins of small animals that he had dried and cured and kept for trading.

James and John were proud of their mother as she stood with John Patterson before Mr. Tom. She looked as pretty as a wild Irish rose in her wedding finery. Her bright auburn hair kept escaping in soft tendrils from the linen cap that she had brought across the sea. Over her gray homespun wedding dress she wore an embroidered white tow apron, and a golden brooch John Patterson had given her pinned together the snowy-white kerchief at her throat.

John Patterson took her hand in his and stood tall and strong beside her as Mr. Tom opened his Bible and the wedding service began. After the bride and groom had taken their vows, a happy celebration followed with feasting and laughter and rejoicing.

Later in the day when Running Deer announced that he would be returning to his village, Mr. Tom and the boys, Mother and the Pattersons all gathered around the Seneca brave to bid him farewell.

Running Deer looked at John and said, "Good-bye, Little Player of Music."

At first John was puzzled by Running Deer calling him that name. Then he remembered the smile that had crossed the young brave's face that stormy night when he had watched John playing the jew's harp.

As Running Deer turned to leave, John called out, "Wait!" And reaching into his bosom pocket, he brought out the jew's harp and pressed it into the Seneca's hand. "I want you to have this for bringing us safely to Mother," he said.

The Indian's dark eyes shone as he looked from the

jew's harp to the boy. "Running Deer thanks white boy for gift," he said solemnly. "Will make fine music for my people." And with that he turned and, like a silent shadow, disappeared into the forest.

At the end of the happy day when the last of the guests had left, the new family and Mr. Tom joined together by the hearth and talked.

"One of the settlers told me that in the spring a church will be built here and you'll have a regular preacher," Mr. Tom told them.

Mother said, "With more and more settlers coming, a school will be built here, too, and a road to connect the settlements."

"You'll soon have your own town right here in the Shenango Valley," replied Mr. Tom, smiling.

"Thank goodness we'll not have to build a fort," John Patterson spoke up. "Chief Cornplanter is a fine man and the Senecas who live in the forest around us are our friends. It is good that we can live in peace with our neighbors."

James looked at John Patterson with shining eyes. The words he had spoken had a familiar ring to the boy and the memory of them stirred his heart. That was what Father had wanted when he had brought his family to America—to live in peace with his neighbors. They were the last words Father had spoken.

James looked around him at the little gathering before the fire—at Mother and John Patterson, at Mr. Tom and Johnny's smiling face. How happy Father would be if he could see them now, James thought. He would be as happy as they all were this night in the Shenango Valley.

A Postscript from the Author

James and John Graham, ancestors of my husband, were real boys. Their father died at sea on the voyage from Northern Ireland to America. Because of lack of money, their mother went on to Pittsburgh alone where she found work as a housekeeper to John Patterson.

Mary Graham left her sons in the care of a Philadelphia family, but because the boys were badly treated, they ran away. They managed to get a ride over the mountains but when they arrived in Pittsburgh, they could not find their mother. Later, when they finally found her in present-day Mercer County, they arrived just in time for her marriage to John Patterson. It was a happy reunion and has been talked about for five generations.

The details of what happened in Philadelphia and during the long journey over the mountains had to be filled in by my imagination. But most of the kind settlers and Indians who helped the travelers along the way were actual people living along the wilderness roads and trails in 1800. Among these good people were John McDowell (the blacksmith), Samuel Semples, George Adams, Adam Brown, the Roberts', the Shawnees at Shawnee Cabins, and the Senecas at Cushcushking.

Mr. Tom is a character created from my own imagination, but many kind and adventuresome circuit riders such as he brought hope, cheer, and the Word of God to the lonely pioneers of the back country.

It wasn't long before the Shenango settlement grew large enough to have a church, a school, and a road. And by the time Janey Patterson grew up and married James Graham, there was a good-sized town called Greenville at the juncture of the Big and Little Shenango rivers.

Ruth Nulton Moore was born in Easton, Pennsylvania, and now lives in Bethlehem, Pennsylvania, with her husband, a professor of accounting at Lehigh University. They have two sons.

Specializing in English literature, she received a BA from Bucknell University and an MA from Columbia University. She did postgraduate work in education at the University of Pittsburgh.

A former schoolteacher, Mrs. Moore has written poetry and stories for *Children's Activities* and *Jack and Jill*. One of her stories has been adapted in an elementary school reader (*High and Wide*, Book 3-1, American Book Company, 1968) and several reading workbooks. She is author of *Frisky, the Playful Pony*, published by Criterion and translated into Swedish by Walstroms Bokforlag; *Hiding the Bell*, published by Westminster Press; and *Peace Treaty*,

The Ghost Bird Mystery, Mystery of the Lost Treasure, and *Tomás and the Talking Birds* (also available in Spanish), all published by Herald Press.

When Mrs. Moore is not at her typewriter, she is busy lecturing about the art of writing to students in the public schools and colleges in her area.

84   81
86   82
    88 98

ourney.